Windswept

Book 3
Serendipity Adventure Romance

Anna Lowe

Editing by Lisa Hollett

Cover design by Fiona Jayde

Contents

Other books in this series

Serendipity Adventure Romance

Off the Charts

Uncharted

Entangled

Windswept

Adrift

www.annalowebooks.com

Free Books

Get your free e-books now!

Sign up for my newsletter at *annalowebooks.com* to get three free books!

- *Desert Wolf*: Friend or Foe (Book 1.1 in the Twin Moon Ranch series)

- *Off the Charts* (the prequel to the Serendipity Adventure series)

- *Perfection* (the prequel to the Blue Moon Saloon series)

Chapter One

"Is everyone ready for another great adventure?" the gray-haired divemaster cried out.

Mia grinned as eight enthusiastic guests replied, "Yes!"

"Is everyone ready for the best dive here in Bonaire, scuba capital of the world?"

"Yes!"

Hans winked at Mia and went on with his trademark line. "Are you ready to rock and roll?"

"Yes!"

The dive launch motored out over the turquoise water, bumping gently over the afternoon ripples in the sheltered bay.

"Okay, everybody, please welcome our crew today," Hans continued. "We've got the lovely Mia, an experienced dive instructor from New York."

Mia pushed a few errant strands of sandy blond hair back from her face, gave a little wave, and went on checking gear without bothering to correct her boss. She'd only lived in New York for a short time before heading to the Caribbean, and that was a time she'd rather forget.

"Not only is Mia a divemaster, she's a sailor, too," Hans went on. "She's sailing her boat around the Caribbean!"

Appreciative *oohs* and *aahs* went out from the guests, and Mia couldn't resist a fond glance toward *Serendipity*, moored on the far side of the bay.

"You have your own boat?" Brenda asked, her eyes big and wide. "Which one is it?"

1

Mia blushed a little and covered up by brushing her hair into a ponytail. Good thing perfect hair wasn't a prerequisite for the job because she was windswept as always, a mess even before her dive.

She pointed to the graceful sloop anchored in the distance. "It was my grandfather's boat," she explained. "He left it to us."

"How long are you in the Caribbean for?" Marc leaned in.

"Three months, maybe four."

An appreciative murmur went up from the guests.

"Plenty of time," Marc said.

Mia nodded. She might not have covered a lot of ground on *Serendipity* yet, but she and her sister were off to a good start. Three months was plenty of time to explore the islands, live a few adventures, and soak in the sun. Plenty of time to forget Mister Tall, Dark, and Hunksome, who'd turned out to be a real jerk.

"We're lucky to have Mia filling in for us this week," Hans finished.

She felt like the lucky one. When Hans had offered her the use of one of the dive shop moorings in exchange for helping out with the occasional dive trip, she'd jumped at the chance.

"And speaking of lucky, meet Lucky, our captain today," Hans added.

"Hi, Lucky!" eight guests sang on cue. Or maybe seven, because the last-minute addition to the trip, a man sitting near the stern, sat quietly withdrawn in the shade of his hoodie.

"Hello, everyone!" Lucky turned from the wheel just long enough to smile broadly: a flash of ivory against his dark skin.

"Lucky's back on Bonaire after several years abroad. Lucky, what's Bonaire's best dive site?"

"The one we're heading to right now!"

Everyone cheered. Everyone but the last-minute guest, who remained hidden away, quietly tapping one foot. Maybe he was nervous. Hans said the man had aced the obligatory check-out dive that morning, but you never knew. Mia made a mental note to keep a close eye on him when the dive began. Which wouldn't be hard given that steely physique.

"Mia, why don't you introduce everyone for Stanley while we motor to the dive site?" Hans asked.

"Yes, Mia, please!" Stanley said, swinging his video camera her way.

She stuck on a smile. Anything for a paying guest, right?

"Sure," she started. "We've got Stanley and Brenda, happy honeymooners from Detroit."

Stanley swung the camera toward his curvy wife. "Love you, honey!"

"Love you, too!" Brenda blew a kiss into the lens.

Love. Mia used to believe in it, too.

She shuffled between the gear that cluttered the center of the launch and motioned toward the next two guests.

"And we have Dirk and Anna from the Netherlands," she continued, "on their twelfth trip to Bonaire."

"Thirteenth," Anna and Dirk said at the same time.

Mia sighed a little inside. There'd been a time when she'd kidded herself into thinking she might have been headed into that kind of relationship. But it hadn't exactly worked out that way.

"They're on home territory." Hans smiled. "This island does belong to Holland, after all."

Mia nodded. That's what she loved about Bonaire: the European flavor sprinkled over the lush Caribbean flair. The island had a culture all its own.

"Thirteen times?" Stanley whistled.

"Lucky number thirteen," the next guest joked.

Mia introduced him for the camera. "Bruno from Switzer-land..."

Bruno waved.

"...and his partner, Marc."

Marc threw a thin arm over Bruno's wide shoulders and squeezed into the shot. "Hi, Stanley!"

"Then we have Pete, also from the Netherlands, who's just completed his dive course with Hans."

Hans gave the young man a hearty thumbs-up. "Never had a student learn so fast."

He said that about all his students, but he meant it every time.

"Which brings me to Hans," she said, "chief diver and owner of Calypso Dives on Bonaire for the past twenty-six years."

He winked. "Which makes my business how much older than you, Mia?"

"Younger, Hans. Your business is younger than me by two years."

Hans always seemed to get a kick out of that.

"Why don't you introduce yourself for the camera, Hans?" she prompted.

"Well…" Hans winked. "I was born in Holland a long, long time ago, but I swear I'll die on Bonaire. Just not anytime soon, I hope!"

Everyone laughed. Even Mia, who'd heard the joke before. His good humor just did that to a person.

"And our last guest today—" she nodded toward the late arrival "—is…"

She watched as he lifted his hands toward the hood. Strong, tough, tanned hands that suggested he spent a lot of time outdoors chopping wood or scoring touchdowns or wrestling Bengal tigers or some such thing. He was bare-chested under that hoodie, as a stack of perfectly sculpted abs showed. Too bad Mia had sworn off men, because this one could have featured in a pinup calendar: *Scorching Hot Divers of the World.*

Then he threw the hood back, and everything in her screeched to a halt. The kind of stop that comes when you slam into a brick wall after roaring along at full speed. Her breath, her circulation, her thoughts — all on pause.

God, please. No. Not him.

Because she knew those piercing green eyes. The ruffled brown hair. The strong, square jaw. She knew every curve of his face, every contour of that hard body just as well as he knew hers.

In other words, intimately.

A little sigh went up from the female guests at the sight of that face.

"Hello, Mia," he said in a voice so low, it might have been a whisper.

"You. . . you. . . you. . ." She scrambled for something to say.

Stanley leaned in with the camera. Mia wasn't sure who she was closer to punching, Stanley or her ex-lover.

Probably her ex-lover. Her Navy-SEAL-turned-New-York-City-cop ex-lover. The one who hadn't bothered sharing those minor details of his life in the four weeks they'd been together.

Four sizzling weeks. Four fun weeks. Possibly the best weeks of her life. He'd swept her right off her feet without even trying, and she'd fallen for him from day one.

Right now, though, her hand squeezed into a fist. The tiny bump where his nose had once been broken — the only imperfection on that striking face — made a handy target.

"Ryan," she managed.

"Mia," he replied, equally tight-lipped.

The camera swung between them, and she might just have swatted it away if Mother Nature hadn't intervened.

"Dolphins!" someone cried, and everyone jumped up to look the other way.

Everyone but Mia, who kept up her death stare, and Ryan, who maintained his unwavering gaze.

"Have you come all the way to Bonaire to embarrass me some more?" she muttered above the noise of the outboard.

Ryan jerked his head from side to side. "I've come all the way to Bonaire to apologize."

She barked a humorless laugh and leaned over him. Good thing she was standing and he was sitting; it was easier to pretend she was imposing that way.

"Right. Apologize. Do it," she dared him.

"I'm sorry, Mia."

He said the words solemnly, but she just scoffed.

"Great. A quiet apology, so nobody notices. Try it loud sometime, Ryan, so everyone can hear. Lay yourself bare. Embarrass yourself as badly as you can, and you still won't know what it was like for me. How humiliating."

She'd never considered heaving a guest overboard, but she sure as hell was tempted now. And with all the adrenaline rushing through her system, she probably could lift his hundred and eighty pounds of muscle over the rail.

"I never meant to hurt you," he murmured, and damn it if his voice didn't stir something inside.

"My humiliation was public, Ryan." She tried to control the shake in her voice, because he didn't deserve to affect her like that. "Out there for everyone to see. To laugh at." Her gut lurched just at the memory.

His eyes flashed and the lines on his brow drew tight. "Believe me, they stopped laughing real quick."

"Oh, yes? When was that? I didn't hear you protesting at the time."

"Mia, I—"

She put a hand up. "I'm not listening to this. I'm finished with your games." She smacked her hands together right in front of his face. "Finished."

"I don't play games."

"Sure. Except with my heart."

His lips tightened, and his back went ramrod straight. Good. Maybe the man had feelings, after all. Maybe he could be made to suffer just a little bit, like her.

"Mia, I—"

She turned her back and started checking dive tanks while the others squealed at the cavorting dolphins.

"Look!" Brenda cried. "The dolphins are going right over to that ship!"

"What is that funny boat?" Marc asked.

Mia kept her eyes down, fighting tears. Who cared what that funny boat was?

"That's *Neptune's Revenge,*" Hans said, gesturing toward the rust-streaked ship. "It's the flagship of one of those extreme environmental groups, The Knights of Neptune."

"The kind that stop whalers?" Brenda asked.

"Whalers, oil rigs, you name it," Hans said.

Mia took another step forward. Another step away from the last man she ever expected to see here. But damn it, her legs were slow to obey, like they were still trapped in his magic spell. Being around Ryan always seem to turn off the thinking part of her mind. Her body was hot all over, her nostrils flaring as if to capture his scent and possess that little bit of him one more time.

Maybe she could sic *Neptune's Revenge* on Ryan. Maybe that would do the trick.

She moved in short, jerky steps that had nothing to do with the gentle motion of the boat until she finally reached Lucky at the bow.

"Everything good, Mia?" As usual, Lucky hadn't missed a thing.

"Peachy."

Situation normal, she decided. All fucked up.

Chapter Two

Sorry.

So easy to say, so difficult to convince somebody of.

Ryan pulled in a deep breath, just as he had the last time Mia turned her back on him, a month earlier in New York. Every muscle in her lean body was stiff, her fists clenched. He'd been hoping four weeks would wear the edges off her anger, but maybe she needed a little more time.

Say, another sixty or seventy years.

The anger was just the surface part, though. Under that was pain, and that's the part he couldn't live with. He hadn't just pissed Mia off, he'd hurt her. It didn't matter that the terrible words she'd overheard weren't meant the way she took them, because the damage was done.

He raked his fingers through his hair, watching Mia hurry away. With the bounce gone from her step, her blond ponytail barely swayed. Her finely chiseled swimmer's shoulders were stiff, but even so, he couldn't rip his eyes away. She walked the way she swam: smooth and silent, toned arms and long legs gliding gracefully along. A class of their own: that was Mia.

A good thing those dolphins had come along; he'd come close to knocking the video camera out of Stanley's hand.

"You can hear them talking!" someone cried out, delighting in the dolphins' antics.

Sure enough, he could just hear the high-pitched squeaks and clicks. A joyous sound that ought to bring a smile to a person's face, but Mia barely seemed to notice.

Mia. Upbeat, optimistic Mia, frowning. Christ, was he the one responsible for that?

"Dolphins have a complex system of communication," Hans said and launched into a long explanation that had Stanley swinging the camera between him and the dolphins. "They're very empathetic, for starters."

Mia shot a pointed glare in Ryan's direction, then went back to checking equipment.

Yeah, he could probably learn a thing or two from dolphins. Maybe if he squeaked at Mia long enough, she'd squeak back. But she was buttoned up tight as a winter coat, so it was all up to him. Which pretty much meant he was doomed, because the only kind of communications the Navy had taught him were things like A was for Alpha, B was for Bravo, C was for Charlie and F... F was all fucked up.

A little like him.

A little like Mia, too.

She hid it so well, he'd had no clue there was an old wound there until he'd managed to reopen it and set off this whole drama. A drama that wasn't supposed to happen, because that was pretty much the only thing they'd both made clear from the start.

I'm only in New York short-term, Mia had said, right after their second or third kiss.

Too bad, he'd said before diving straight into the next kiss, because a couple of touches of those amazing lips were never going to be enough. *But short-term probably works better for me, too.*

Yeah, he'd been that dumb. Thinking that a couple of weeks with Mia would be enough, just like a couple of weeks with any one woman had always proven to be enough. But if Mia had been just any woman, he wouldn't be in Bonaire right now.

In Bonaire, fucking up completely. Again.

For all that he'd planned out his apology, he still hadn't gotten it right. He looked over the side of the boat, wondering if dolphins ever found themselves in his position. They probably kept things simple, though, like he thought he could do when he first met her.

So, what do you do? she'd asked, that first brunch they went out to after a week of swimming laps beside each other at the local pool. A week of her kicking everyone's ass, including his, then climbing out of the pool like it was any other Sunday. And hell, the way she swam, maybe that was her average Sunday: starting off with ninety minutes of churning laps, making the local boys look like doggie paddlers before hopping out of the water, dripping from every lean curve of her body. Never had the five-to-six a.m. time slot drawn so many eager swimmers to the pool.

He'd dragged his eyes from her animated face after that innocent question and stared into his coffee for a while. Did he really want to dwell on his job?

Work has been a little... all-consuming lately. I'd rather talk about other stuff.

It's not that he was burned out or anything. Just that he wasn't exactly... *not* burned out.

When Mia reached a hand across the table and put it over his, a little electric zing ran through his body like she'd just closed a high-voltage circuit and let the juice flow. And instead of starting off on some sappy girl talk about how important it was to talk things through, she'd let her summer blue eyes go soft while she started a discussion of the misadventures of a long line of basset hounds she'd grown up with. Made him grin and chuckle and laugh and all the other things he hadn't done enough of lately.

We had Sherlock first, and he got skunked the very night we had to rush to my sister's ballet recital...

Over the next hour, his facial muscles had gotten the kind of workout he whipped the rest of his body through six times a week.

Then we got Bella, and she had puppies, but she was the worst mother ever. Good thing she was low to the ground, because she'd get up and walk away while the puppies were nursing and they'd all drag along...

And damn if that hadn't spurred him into talking about the time his scrappy mutt King had run off with the neighbor's poodle and a lot of other stories he hadn't thought about in ages. Funny things. Lighthearted things. Good things he'd somehow forgotten.

And just like that, an unspoken pact was born. They'd meet, swim their laps together, go to brunch on days they had off, and never, ever discuss work. Not his, not hers. Even when they started wrapping up brunch with a kiss instead of a wave goodbye, they didn't talk about work. And definitely not once they started taking brunch to her place. And when brunch at her place turned into sex at her place, well, why talk shop? There was so much else to talk about, and so much else to do other than talk.

Like gazing into those bottomless blue eyes that could cycle through the seasons in a single day. Like watching her lope through each hour as if it might hold a wonderful new adventure. Like wondering if some things weren't too good to be true.

They'd gone a month like that, and it was perfect. Getting to wake up with her snuggled up close. Touching her silky hair. Listening to her breathe quietly, then watching her wake up and look at him like it was perfect for her, too.

Until the morning he turned up for one of those required dive refresher courses with the squad, and surprise, surprise. Guess who was the instructor?

Mia. Mia with her long eyelashes and pink cheeks and way of tilting her head that could drive a man crazy in the very best way. But stupid him — one offhand comment and everything had fallen apart.

In the weeks that followed, he'd pushed the boundaries of police regulations to track her down, but finally, he'd figured out where she'd disappeared to. And here he was in Bonaire, trying to deliver an apology. Maybe even trying to win her back. But doing that on a dive boat with nine other people crowded around... Okay, not one of his better ideas. He puffed out a long breath.

Sorry was really not cutting it. So he'd have to try harder, right?

"Oh, look!" Brenda called. "I think there's a baby dolphin back there!"

Everyone in the boat came rushing over, and in the excitement, Ryan managed to work his way to a new spot across from Mia, behind Lucky the driver.

"Looks like it's gonna be a hell of a day!" Lucky said, waving a hand over the bay.

"Yeah," he murmured. "Sure does."

Chapter Three

Mia counted every dragging minute up to the moment Lucky throttled down and approached the dive site. A good thing, too, because another second of Ryan's imploring eyes on her back and she might just lose her mind.

"Stanley, get some footage of that Neptune boat." Brenda nudged her husband. "Maybe we'll see them on TV someday."

Mia gave the environmental activists' flagship a passing glance. The converted freighter had been anchored there all week, a familiar feature of the landscape by now. Just like *Serendipity,* floating serenely on the far side of the bay. If she strained her eyes, she might just be able to make out the mast. The temptation to jump overboard and swim for home was hard to resist, even if it was two miles away. She could curl into a ball in the cabin and wish Ryan away.

The distance didn't deter her; only her pride did. That, and she had a job to do. She leaned over the side and made short work of catching the mooring ball and making the dive boat fast, trying to collect her scattered nerves.

Hans was about to start the dive brief, and all eyes jumped to him. All but the emerald green pair fixed firmly on her. Eyes that said, *Listen, Mia. Hear me out.*

Except Ryan wasn't saying anything, and she wasn't about to listen even if he did. That tortured warrior look on his face was probably just for show, right?

Please, his eyes begged.

She turned her back and checked the mooring line. Again.

"Okay, folks!" Hans clapped for attention. "We've got a hell of a dive for you today!" He took out a small whiteboard and started narrating in his light Dutch accent. "We dive here and proceed slowly to the bow end of the wreck of the *Henry Aalders,* twenty-five meters down. That's eighty feet for our American friends."

Stanley leaned over the rail and pointed his camera into the clear water. Even at this depth, Mia could see the faint outline of the wreck.

"We'll follow the mooring line down and explore the deeper end of the wreck — as deep as forty meters, or one hundred and thirty feet."

The Swiss couple checked their matching dive computers.

"That's deep, folks. It's critical that you stay with your divemasters — that's me and Mia. You can't miss us. I'm the handsome one in black neoprene, and she's the homely one in pink."

That drew some laughs, along with looks from the male guests that assured Mia she was anything but homely. She zipped the upper portion of her pink-and-purple wetsuit up. Way up. Yeah, she had an okay body, but that feeling of people looking — really looking — made her skin crawl. Too many bad memories from a long time ago.

And some from not so long ago, too. Her gaze slid to Ryan then vaulted away.

"We're at slack tide now, but as soon as it starts to turn, the current will set in, and we don't want anyone to wander away. Okay?"

"Okay!" The guests nodded. All except Ryan, who studied her with those earnest eyes.

"After diving to those depths, we'll have to make decompression stops on the way up. Serious stuff, folks." Hans' face went grave, as it did every time he emphasized the point. "If you come up too quickly, you can get hurt."

Everyone went silent.

"I've seen a man die of the bends, and I never want to see that again," he added, looking each guest in the eye. "So, safety first. We come up nice and slow, all right?"

Eight somber heads nodded in unison. Even Ryan. Especially Ryan, who'd never seemed as serious as he did right now.

Lucky was the only one who didn't seem to be listening. Mia followed his gaze to another dive launch moored not too far away. A small boat carrying two men, one of whom was going over the side, kitted out like he was going to the center of the Earth. Another camera junkie, probably.

"All right, everybody buddy up and follow me." Hans pointed. "Stanley and Brenda, check?"

"Check!"

"Marc and Bruno, check?"

"Check!"

"Dirk and Anna, check?"

"Check!"

"Pete, you're with me."

Pete gave a double thumbs-up.

"And Ryan..."

Mia felt her stomach sink. She made chopping motions in the air, hoping Hans would catch on.

He didn't, of course. "Ryan, you can buddy with Mia, who'll bring up the rear."

Ryan's lips barely moved. "Check," he said, looking like a badass soldier about to march off on a heroic mission that defied all odds.

Which fit, because as it turned out, he was a badass soldier, or had been before becoming a badass New York cop.

She risked another glance in his direction, and damn it, his Mission Impossible eyes were still on her. The scary thing was, they said his mission was *her*.

She steeled her shoulders just like she used to do, staring down a tough opponent before a swim start. *You, mister, are about to meet your match.*

Or so she hoped, because her pride couldn't afford to cave in to him again.

Getting the guests in the water took forever, and Mia suspected the dive would feel torturously long, too. Stanley took ages getting the waterproof housing on his camera. Marc fiddled with the anti-fog in his mask. Pete checked everything three times, just as Hans taught him. Ryan pulled his wetsuit up, and even in skintight neoprene — especially in skintight neoprene — he looked like a sex on a stick.

Hans moved around the launch, checking every regulator, every O ring. Lucky remained at the bow, his restless eyes roving the bay. One after the other, the guests donned their fins and splashed into the sea until it was just her and Ryan alone on the stern platform, squeezed into a tiny space.

"Mia," he started. "I meant it. I'm sorry."

She squeezed her lips into a thin line. She'd feel better when the regulator was in his mouth, because the bass in his voice could do wicked things to her resolve.

"Ready for your dive, Mr. Hayes?"

His cheek twitched. Yeah, he got the message.

"Ready if you are, Ms. Whitman."

"Then jump in already." *Before I shove you in.*

He looked at her for another second — just looked, like he wanted to reach out and stroke her cheek like he used to do. Slow and tender, one finger would trace the curve of her face, then glide back up the length of her jaw to do it again, making her warm all over.

She flushed and stepped back. Way back.

A pained expression flashed across Ryan's face before he went back to neutral. Then he turned away from her, covered his mask with one hand and the top of his tank with the other, and stepped expertly off the stern.

Navy SEAL. NYPD dive squad. Recent lover.

Mia shook her head at herself. Holy shit.

She fiddled with her mask much longer than she needed to.

"Everything okay?" Lucky asked.

She didn't need to look up to know he was watching her with concern.

"Fine," she mumbled into her mask. It was business as usual, right?

She patted her vest in a last check, took the deepest breath of her life, and jumped in.

Chapter Four

The water was unusually clear for afternoon, and the sun slanted through the upper layer, splitting into a thousand fingers of light just like it would in a centuries-old cathedral. Mia exhaled slowly as she descended, creating a stream of bubbles that tickled her ear on their way to the surface. They popped among the silver-white wavelets rippling overhead. She spun in a slow circle, taking it all in. Even with the limited peripheral vision of her dive mask, the intense blues and the sideways light seemed endless, a universe of its own. Mia had logged hundreds of dives all over the world, but the sight never failed to fill her with awe.

She continued her slow turn and found Ryan watching her from five feet away. Even underwater and through a dive mask, even with the intense aquamarine of the water, the green of his eyes stood out.

Fine. It would be fine. He was just another dive buddy on just another dive, right?

She curled her fingers in the "okay" signal, and he did the same.

She used to have a fantasy that looked a lot like this, back when they were first getting to know each other. To take Ryan to a tropical island and share the wonders of diving with him. Little did she know he was a diver, too. And not just any diver, but a pro.

This looked just like that fantasy, but it didn't feel anything like it. There was no joy, no anticipation. Just a gnawing dread.

The group was strung out ahead, some deep, others still working out the pressure in their ears. She caught up with Brenda and spent a minute in quiet support at her side. Usually, that was all it took: steady eye contact and a confident "okay" sign to settle a novice's nerves. Stanley was wandering off to the right, but Ryan herded him subtly back in, sticking close to the man's right side.

She could see Ryan's experience as clearly as she could see Stanley's lack thereof. Ryan floated sideways in perfect neutral buoyancy, his body completely relaxed. He might have been a lazy Roman, stretched out on a couch and nibbling on grapes. Stanley, on the other hand, bobbed up and down like a bath toy with every clumsy adjustment to his air vest. The bubbles that rose from Ryan's regulator with each exhale were small and measured; Stanley's erupted in great bursts, then trickled off.

Hans waited for everyone to regroup at the wreck before giving them the okay to explore sign. Mia followed Brenda and Stanley while everyone else explored around the far side of the sunken freighter. Everyone except Ryan, of course. She wished she could shake him off, but he was her goddamn buddy now.

Her sleek, muscled buddy who moved as effortlessly in the water as he did on land. Or in bed.

Which she was absolutely, positively, not going to think about at a time like this. Or any other time, because it was over between them. Over.

Over, over, over. She repeated the mantra as a parrotfish swam by in a flash of green and blue.

Brenda slowly relaxed into the dive. Stanley doubled back to photograph the view through a porthole in the wreck. Ryan was two strokes ahead, honing in on a colony of pink and green anemones, so Mia backtracked to stay behind Stanley.

She did a slow scan to make sure they hadn't lost anyone, and a good thing, too, because one diver was heading off in the opposite direction. Bruno? Marc? She couldn't tell who. Only that the diver was going the wrong way, fast. What had gotten into him?

There was no time to alert Hans or anyone else; she had to act quickly to catch up with the diver and bring him back. She started kicking after the man and cursing inside. What was that idiot thinking, getting so far away from the group?

Mia always prided herself on ending a dive with air to spare, using slow, steady breaths, but this errant diver was forcing her to work hard to catch up. She was going to have a stern word with Bruno or Marc or whoever this was once they got back to the launch.

The bottom sloped away and the man followed it deeper and deeper. She followed with ever more urgent kicks, despite the pressure building in her ears. One hundred and thirty-five feet was fine for recreational divers, but this guy was pushing a hundred and forty-five. She glanced at her dive watch. One hundred and fifty. Christ, what was he after, thundering along like that?

The man was quick, probably thanks to those new model UltraFlow fins she'd been coveting in the pages of the latest dive magazines. She was faster, but it still took long minutes to pull within reach of those fins. About a minute too long, because he was breaking one hundred and sixty feet by then. Getting him back to the group was out of the question now. She'd have to lead him to the surface in a slow, controlled ascent and get him to the dive boat on her own.

Diving is perfectly safe, her first divemaster used to say. *Only stupidity makes it dangerous.* Case in point: the diver in front of her now.

She kicked into a sprint, grabbed the edge of his vest, and pulled back just hard enough to make sure he got the message. Yeah, she was pissed. Bruno or Marc or whoever it was totally out of line, and he should know it.

A violent burst of bubbles showed his surprise as he spun to face her with wide eyes.

Mia blinked.

Those wide, angry eyes that didn't belong to Bruno or Marc or anyone else from her group. Neither did the gray vest or blue hooded wetsuit. Who was this guy? What was he doing, diving so deep and on his own?

The eyes flashed with surprise before narrowing on hers, and the stranger huffed through his mouthpiece. *What the hell?*

She wanted to huff back. She had every right to ask him that.

He shoved her away. Really shoved, and she was stunned by the brute force of it. Then he twisted, folding his body to grab something near his leg. When he straightened, something silver flashed in his hand.

A knife. A knife slashing toward her in a terrifyingly slow-motion kind of way.

Chapter Five

A knife? A dive knife?

Mia screamed into her mask, and it came out in a burst of bubbles. She clawed at the water in an attempt to back away.

Too late — the man grabbed her shoulder with one hand and slashed with the other. A flood of bubbles exploded in her face as the regulator was ripped from her mouth, streaming a curtain of air into the water.

She kicked and flailed, screaming inside. Was he trying to kill her?

The knife slashed again, saying, *Yes. Yes, I am.*

She jerked right, a hair away from the jagged blade.

Oh my God, oh my God...

She kicked in reflex, struck him along the ribs, and ripped free. Flailing all four limbs, she backed away from the furious eyes of a madman.

He clutched at the water between them, and between the wild trail of bubbles flying everywhere, she could see the curse in his eyes. Then, with an angry shake of his head, the man jackknifed backward and torpedoed into the indigo depths.

Mia forced herself not to panic. To do what she'd taught countless students over the years: dip one shoulder and reach behind with one hand to retrieve the dislodged regulator and bring it back to her mouth.

With her vision restricted by her mask, all she could do was grope blindly behind her until — salvation! — her hand met the hose and traced it to the mouthpiece. She thrust it back into her mouth and sucked in a lungful of air.

23

You got this. You got this under control.

But she didn't have anything under control, and she knew it. Bubbles were shooting up all around her like a whole squad of divers had surrounded her to exhale at the same time. At least the mystery diver was fading out of sight, kicking urgently onward, undeterred.

She glanced down toward her chest, patting at the hoses and her vest. What was wrong with her regulator? Why was it dumping so much air?

She traced the backup regulator and brought it into sight. It kicked and jumped in her hand like a garden hose gone wild, disgorging a steady stream of air.

Her air. Jesus, he'd cut through the hose!

She grabbed her tank display and cupped it in front of her face like a holy relic.

Her air level was halfway down and dropping fast. And here she was, one hundred and sixty feet down.

She looked up. The sun was pale and distant, as it might have looked from a distant planet in the solar system. One hundred and sixty feet was a hell of a long way.

Every instinct told her to shoot for the surface, but she fought the panic down.

It was too far. Shooting to the surface meant death.

Hans' words echoed in her mind. *I've seen a man die of the bends, and I never want to see that again.*

She could imagine it all too well. By breathing compressed air, she'd been pumping tiny particles of oxygen into her bloodstream. If she ascended too quickly, those bubbles would steadily expand until they burst inside her. They'd rupture her arteries and kill her in the most horrible way.

She fumbled with the cut end of the hose, trying to stem the flood of pressurized air. Her fingers fumbled to fold it. *Quick! Quick!* But the hose jumped free and sprayed her surroundings with a crazy line of bubbles that might have been pretty if it hadn't meant her life.

She grabbed at the hose again and kicked upward, fighting back the panic. There was no way the remaining air would last her to the surface. The only safe way up was slowly, making decompression stops along the way. One hundred and sixty feet... she'd need at least two stops along the way.

Jesus, she was going to be Hans' worst nightmare. Her own worst nightmare. Every diver's worst nightmare.

Up! Up! Up! instinct screamed.

Slow!

No, fast! Now!

She dumped a little air out of her buoyancy vest and regretted it right away, watching the bubbles shoot past. God, she was stupid! That was the equivalent of a desert wanderer letting the last drop of water tip out of a canteen.

Think, Mia! Think!

But she couldn't think. She started kicking upward. Just ten feet, then she'd check her air.

One hundred thirty feet. She stared at the air gauge.

Already into the red.

If she waited any longer, she'd drown. If she hurried up, she'd be torn asunder from the inside out.

Something in her snapped and she started kicking upward. Drowning was a given if she stayed down, but she might have a tiny chance of survival if the dive team got her to a decompression chamber on time. If the dive team noticed her at all. If her body could somehow hold out. If...

She kicked upward, but her fin caught on something. She glanced down and nearly spit out her regulator. The crazed diver was back, and he was pulling her down. He took firm hold of her fin and yanked. She could already picture the knife in his other hand. He'd slash and stab and leave a trail of blood to join the last bubbles trickling out of her tank. Even if that didn't kill her, the sharks would be on her in an instant and—

The man jerked her foot so hard, her fin nearly came off. She kicked back in self-defense, launching all kinds of crazy plans. Maybe she could knock his regulator out of his mouth and take it for herself. Maybe she could—

He pulled harder, and nothing she tried worked against that brute strength. The man was forcing her down, working his way up her body until they were nearly mask-to-mask.

She sucked in a lungful of air, ready to kick him hard, but there was no air. Her lungs grabbed at nothingness. The tank was empty. Her air was out. Worse, his hands clamped over her wrists and locked them together.

He really was crazy. He really did want to kill her.

She flexed her knee to slam him in the balls, but her legs were tangled with his and it didn't work. She glared because that was all she had left. Glaring, then dying. Would he watch as she gulped water and slowly drowned? Would he push her away like a flopping fish? Would that evil face—

He shook her a little, and she blinked.

It wasn't the man who'd attacked her. The man locking both her hands in one of his wore a black wetsuit, not a blue one like the man with the knife. He was bigger. Stronger.

Familiar.

She blinked again. His eyes were deep. Intense. Worried.

Green eyes. . . .not her attacker.

Ryan.

If she'd had any air left, she would have cried.

Chapter Six

Ryan pulled his regulator out and guided it toward Mia's mouth, telling himself it would be all right. Just like he'd told himself on the long flight from New York to Bonaire and during the interminable hours going from dive shop to dive shop to track her down. Somehow, it would be all right. She'd listen and forgive him and everything would be all right.

But fuck, who was he trying to kid? They were one hundred and thirty feet down with less than half a tank of air between the two of them.

Damned if he knew how that happened, other than he'd turned from Stanley to see Mia sprinting off after another diver. A diver who'd attacked her when she got close. Every instinct screamed for him to go after the man and exact his revenge, but that would mean leaving Mia, and he couldn't do that.

Calm down, he willed her to understand. *Breathe easy.*

Her eyes were jumping all over the place, but at least she'd quit trying to claw her way to the surface. That would be certain death, and both of them knew it.

Eye contact. That was the key. He had to keep her focus on him and not on the odds, which were pretty fucking slim.

So he channeled all kinds of calm juju her way and hoped she'd gotten enough air, because he sure as hell would need his regulator back pretty soon.

He ran his hands over her gear and traced her spare hose down to the slashed-off end.

Jesus.

He stuck the end in his mouth and caught the last little trickle of bubbles because, who knew? That might just make the difference in the end. When that tapered off, he concentrated on her eyes and on letting an even trail of bubbles out of his mouth. That was the first thing he'd learned in his first dive course with the Navy all those years ago: no holding your breath when using compressed air. It was either breathing in or breathing out. In or out. And right now, with Mia sucking on his air like a shisha pipe, his only choice was out.

She clamped two hands over his regulator and sucked like she was never letting go, but gradually, her eyes zoomed in on his and her breathing slowed.

He cursed himself for bringing his old gear to Bonaire — the outdated set with a single regulator and no second breather unit — but it was all he had, and it wasn't like he could bring along one of the NYPD sets for this trip.

Feeling his way along his hip, he pulled his air gauge into view.

Shit.

Even if he had two regulators, the air supply would be awfully tight. Too tight, and Mia was gulping it like a fish.

He made little up and down motions. *Slow down. Slow down.* Then he flicked his fingers toward his face. If he didn't get any air soon, she'd be the one dragging his body to shore.

She took a last drag of air and pushed the regulator at him, and though he'd told himself he wouldn't be greedy, it was so sweet, so clear, he couldn't help it. A breath, two breaths, and he passed it back to Mia.

She stuck her thumb up and he nodded. Just like it had always been with them: perfect communication from the first minute they'd met in that pool in New York. Well, perfect communication on some issues. On others... Well, not so good, as it turned out.

Focus, Hayes. Focus.

He fluttered his fins twice and let his body rise, trying to conserve energy. Every kick meant more oxygen used, and they couldn't afford that. He kept a firm grip on the shoulder straps of Mia's vest, too, keeping eye contact. That was the easy part, because her sky blue eyes were like the ocean. He could look and look and never get tired of searching those depths.

If they did survive this — no, *when* they survived this, he decided, because he had to believe — he'd find that maniac diver and rip him limb from limb just so he could piece the guy together and do it all over again.

Breathe in, breathe out. Breathe in, hand over. They had a pattern going now, and Mia's breaths were more controlled. Jesus, the woman was tough. Navy-SEAL tough, and he ought to know. She shot him a little smile when she handed back the regulator, and even if it was forced, it gave him hope. Mia, smiling for him. Maybe if they made it out of this alive, she'd hear him out.

But he'd cross that bridge when he came to it. Right now was about getting her out of this alive.

Everything ticked over in slow motion, even though it was life or death. It was always like that, in the thousands of training exercises and the couple of real-life close calls that he'd always, always aced. Except there never seemed to be as much on the line as right now.

The water muffled all sound and movement. There was nothing but the trail of bubbles, shooting to the surface the way he wished he could. His universe became Mia's face and the air and depth gauges that showed numbers he really didn't want to see but had to face up to if they were going to get out of this alive.

One hundred feet, and running out of air fast.

Eighty. He held her eyes, willing her to ascend slowly.

Sixty. The sunlight grew brighter, teasing and tempting them both.

He tightened his grip on Mia's vest, making sure she ascended slowly past the fifty- and thirty-foot marks.

When they came up on twenty feet, he tugged on her vest. Now came the tricky part: stopping to decompress when the surface seemed so unbearably close. He raised a hand in a stop sign and pointed to his watch.

Her eyes flicked there then back to his face, and her brow tightened.

Yeah, he knew just what she was thinking. They didn't have enough air for a proper ascent with carefully timed decompression stops. Four minutes at twenty feet was what his dive computer was showing as the minimum.

Mia pulled his air gauge over and held up two fingers.

He shook his head and held up four. Two wouldn't do it.

Stubborn as ever, she held up three.

He shook his head again. Four. He'd never ordered her to do anything, but damn it, this wasn't negotiable.

She pointed at the air gauge. *We don't have enough.*

He made little patting motions in the water. *So we'll have to slow our breathing down.*

Her face twisted toward the surface, and he knew just what she was thinking. On a normal dive, either of them could ascend that little bit without any trouble. But they were coming from deep, deep down, and the tiny bubbles in their blood needed a chance to dissipate. Otherwise—

There was no otherwise. There was only death.

He cupped her cheek and brought her eyes back to his. Couldn't help stroking a thumb across her cheek.

Not there. Look here. Look at me.

If she looked at the surface, she might bolt for it, and he couldn't let that happen. They had to take this one step at a time.

Her chest rose, then fell, and she closed her eyes. Took a smaller puff of air this time and handed the regulator back.

He nodded. Small, controlled breaths. If anyone could do it, it was Mia. He pictured her swimming laps in the pool where they'd met. Mia with her perfect breath control and perfect strokes. Perfect everything, like the way she'd carve a flip turn then whiz past him like he was a rookie and not the best swimmer in his squad.

She had a perfect smile, too, and it always felt like she had a deluxe version of it just for him.

At least, that's the way it used to be.

A whole school of barracuda flitted past, all silvery scales and pointed teeth. There'd been a rainbow of fish around the wreck, too, and you'd think that after two years of diving in

New York Harbor, he'd have been entranced. Diving in New York was like submerging yourself in pea soup that had gone sour; here, it was like looking out from a mountaintop on a very clear day. But all he'd had eyes for was Mia. With her hair floating around her head, she looked like a mermaid, and the wavering beams of light cutting through the water all seemed to focus on her. Mia with her determined eyes and taut arms and silky touch. God, she was something.

Focus, damn it!

He glanced at his watch. Three minutes forty seconds down. Three minutes fifty seconds. Three minutes fifty-five. He nodded, and she nodded back. Time to continue the ascent. Slowly, carefully. Or as slowly and carefully as the ticking clock allowed.

Ten feet. Baby depth, really, but not today. His dive computer blinked, signaling a six-minute stop.

Six minutes. An eternity. Especially with the air gauge dipping closer and closer to empty.

Mia had her hands clamped around his vest now, too, and they waited out another interminable stop as close as a couple of intertwined eels. The front of her vest bumped his, and some base part of his mind wished for the alternative: skin to skin, like all the times they'd lain clasped tight in her bed, coming down from another high. Which was probably an inappropriate image, but if he did die, he'd go thinking thoughts like that, because that was a hell of a lot better than imagining bubbles expanding in his bloodstream and killing him from the inside out.

The surface was so close, but he didn't dare look up. Didn't want to check the air gauge, either, but he had to.

Mia must have read it in his face, because she pulled the gauge over and immediately paled. Yeah, it was going to be tight.

He tried doing the calculations. Even with a mind that was a little foggy from lack of air, he knew it was better to wait out the full decompression stop than to rush. Worst case, they could shoot to the surface after the stop...

No, he realized. Worst case, they'd be dead.

No, absolutely worst case, he would live, and Mia would die.

He made his next intake a shorter one and passed the regulator back to her. Whatever calming effect his gaze had on her, she was doing the same for him.

We'll make it through this, her look said. *We'll be okay.*

He risked a slightly deeper breath and nodded. *Okay.*

With every endless second of that decompression stop, the urge to kick to the surface grew, until wrestling that temptation became the fight of his life. If he hadn't been with Mia, he might have even taken the risk and given in to the instinct to rise. But instincts couldn't be trusted, not when it came to diving with compressed air. His Navy days had taught him that, and he sure as hell wasn't going to unlearn it now. Everything came down to calculations and self-control.

Four minutes into the decompression stop, two to go. Air in the red zone. Death hanging over his shoulder, leaning in with a greedy grin.

He inhaled, passed the regulator to Mia, and watched her suck air in, all nice and calm — until her eyes went wide and her hands fluttered. She made chopping motions across her throat and jabbed her thumbs up.

Out of air! Out of air!

Chapter Seven

If it hadn't been for Ryan's insistent grip on her vest, Mia would have shot straight to the surface. But with his hands on her and his eyes, too — calm, bottomless eyes that promised everything would be okay — she kept her last shred of control and ascended slowly.

He flickered his fingers in front of his mouth. *Exhale.*

Right. Exhale, with the lungful of air she never got. She forced a weak trail of bubbles from her lips as she let her body rise, waiting for a ripping feeling to set in as the air in her veins expanded and tore her insides apart.

But there was no tearing, only a burning pain from lungs desperate for air.

Exhale, damn it!

She squeezed another couple of bubbles out of her lungs. Watched the sun grow brighter, the surface nearer. Her lungs screamed for her to open her mouth, but she fought the urge back. That second decompression stop had been too short. Much too short. Somehow, she had to drag this all out.

Almost there...

Ryan's grip tightened on her vest. *Not too fast.*

It was a little like swimming laps next to him, when her body would beg for a break while her pride had her digging for just a little more speed, a little more glide. A little more air.

Another few seconds...

Then she couldn't do it any more. She tore out of his grasp and kicked for her life. Kicked for the surface and a breath of fresh air. Her ears wailed and her lungs burned and her eyes bulged and—

She didn't just shoot to the surface, she shot clear through it and a couple of feet into the air, gasping. The water beside her erupted in a great wave and Ryan was there, too, breaching like a mighty orca. Heaving for breath, they both flopped around like a couple of fish who'd forgotten to swim. She couldn't quite get her inhales and exhales timed right; one started before the other finished, making her cough and splutter and spit. Which really didn't matter, because there was air, dry air, all around her. A whole universe of it. The sun beat down from the sky, and it was a glorious day there on the surface. A glorious day.

Her hand got stuck on something, and it took a minute to comprehend why. Her fingers were laced through Ryan's. Not feeling like they'd let go anytime soon, either.

"You okay?" he gasped.

She managed a weak nod.

He shook his head. "Really okay?"

She touched her own ribs as if that would tell her if she was bursting inside or not. But surely if she was going to die of the bends, she'd feel it, right?

"I'm okay." She nodded. "You?"

His nod was so haggard, she pulled him closer. He'd had less air to go on than her.

"Really okay?" Now she was the one grabbing him by both shoulders, studying him up close. No sign of bleeding around his nose or ears, thank God.

The right side of his mouth curled into a tiny grin. Teensytiny, like it might not be allowed. The same grin that had captivated her from the very start, because Ryan smiling was like a statue coming to life and sensing its surroundings for the very first time.

"I'm okay."

His face was pale, but his eyes were bright, and she gulped the sight in along with huge lungfuls of air. Like she couldn't survive without both.

"Jesus, Mia, what happened?"

Blurry images flooded her mind. The diver. The struggle. The flashing knife. It all welled up until she was gasping as much as when she'd surfaced seconds ago. She shook her head. Not going there now. Definitely not going there.

Her body felt like lead, and her gear seemed twice as heavy as it had been at the start of the dive. She had to get out of the water, fast. Where was Lucky with the dive boat?

"This way," Ryan grunted, tugging her arm.

The small dinghy moored off to the right wasn't the dive launch, but it was the closest thing afloat, and it sure would do for now. She forced her arms into a weak paddling motion. God, if her swim coach saw her now...

Those hundred yards seemed like a thousand, and she had to stop to float on her back twice along the way, but she made it. She grabbed the oar strapped along the side of the dinghy and hung on like her life depended on it. Pressed her forehead against the rubber and made a little cave where she didn't have to see, feel, think, or do anything but breathe. Everything was okay. She was okay.

Ryan was shoulder-to-shoulder with her, a solid, safe mass. Whether it was his proximity or sheer exhaustion that kept her from losing it completely didn't matter right now. Only that she was okay.

His arm circled her shoulders, and that helped, too. The sound of his breath, the warmth of his touch. Him rubbing her back and whispering, *Thank God you're okay.* Touching her, making sure she was all there.

She looped one arm around him and hid her face in his shoulder. Held him tightly and wondered what it was that had ever driven them apart.

A little wave splashed in between them, and she looked up. Right into his eyes, which were filled with a logjam of words that couldn't quite make their way out.

"Where's Lucky when you need him?" he finally murmured, looking around.

She kept her head down, reluctant for Lucky or anyone else to come roaring in right now. Another minute of breathing in

Ryan and she just might forget what had her so mad at him. Forget that little bit of bad and remember all the good.

"There he is." Ryan lifted an arm to wave.

She looked up, scanning the area. *Neptune's Revenge*, the environmental activists' ship, was the biggest thing in sight, and the next nearest thing afloat. Hans' dive launch was a few hundred feet to the right, where she could make out the first guests clambering up the stern, wondering, perhaps, where she and Ryan had wandered off to. Hans would joke it off in front of the guests, but he'd have a stern word with her later. What would she say? Would anyone believe her?

I got mixed up and swam off after a stranger who turned on me with a knife...

The image flashed in her mind, so near and real, she gasped. The man had been face-to-face with her, all anger and frustration. What had she ever done to him?

"Did you see the man?" She gripped Ryan's arm.

His face clouded. "The one who cut your air? I did. And if I'd been a little closer, he'd have had that knife stuck between his ribs."

He meant it, too; she could see it in the flash of his eyes.

"What the hell was he doing, attacking you like that?"

"I don't know. I just swam up, thinking he was one of the guests, and he pulled a knife on me!"

"What kind of guy pulls a knife on another diver?"

She was wondering the same thing. "What kind of guy dives alone at those depths?"

"What was he up to, anyway?"

The words were barely out of Ryan's mouth when a blinding yellow-red flash filled the sky, together with a clap of thunder. Mia was slammed against the dinghy, shaken nearly senseless. Which way was up? Where was Ryan? What was going on?

A strong hand grabbed her vest and pulled her underwater, and she kicked hard, imagining the attacker back for another try. But it wasn't the other diver. It was Ryan, dragging her under the dinghy before letting her pop up on the other side. Keeping an arm over her head like a shield against the fiery bits of... something hailing down on her from above.

The dinghy rocked up and down from a shock wave, but Ryan kept her sheltered long after the roaring in her ears faded. She shook her head, but a dull ring remained along with a steady, crackling noise not too far away. She blinked and peeked out around the shelter of the dinghy.

"Oh my God," she breathed, watching flames lick over the listing hull of *Neptune's Revenge.* "It blew up," she said, feeling numb. "It blew up."

Ryan shook his head. "It was blown up."

"Blown up? But who would do such a thing—" She cut herself off, because she knew. The diver she'd chased down — that's why he attacked her.

The outrage in Ryan's face turned to concern. He touched her cheek, and when he drew back, his fingers were smeared with blood. Her blood?

"Jesus, Mia, are you okay?"

Chapter Eight

It was just a bloody nose caused by being flung against the oar of the dinghy, but nobody would listen. Not Ryan, whose eyes went wide as if Mia were showing the first sign of the bends. Not Lucky, either, or Hans, when they finally honed in on Ryan's shouts and motored the launch over. The flow of blood slowed down by the time she wobbled onboard, but that didn't stop Stanley from zooming in on her face. She might even have smacked the camera out of his hands if it weren't for a comment that stopped her dead in her tracks.

"We can make the evening news with this footage!" he exclaimed.

Evening news. Unexpected camera footage. Of her.

Bile rose in her throat along with memories. A whole lot of ugly memories.

Something at her side moved, cougar-fast, and all the guests cried out.

It was Ryan, snatching the camera out of Stanley's hands. Ryan, leaning over Stanley like a very angry Zeus clutching a lightning bolt. Ryan, stepping to her rescue.

Again.

"Get. The. Camera. Out. Of. Her. Face." He growled it, so low and menacing that everyone went still. Deathly still.

A very silent minute ticked by, finally broken by Stanley's squeaked, "Sorry."

Ryan muttered something and dropped to his knees in front of her, cupping her face with both hands.

"No more diving for you," he murmured, stroking her cheeks with both thumbs. "Not today. Not tomorrow. Not for the rest of the week."

"You can't tell me what to do," she peeped.

He put on that *watch-it-lady*, New York cop thing he did so well and dabbed at her face with a towel. So tenderly that she had the sensation of bubbles expanding in her bloodstream — in a good way. The next thing she knew, she was drooping against his chest. And damn it, she couldn't quite summon the willpower to pull away.

All the way back to shore, Ryan watched her with eyes that swore murder and damnation at anyone who came close. Which included the ambulance crew when they checked her out, and the police, once she was finally proclaimed in good health and hauled to headquarters for questioning.

Wait a minute. Questioning?

She'd barely had a chance to change out of her swimwear before they brought her in, and there she was, blinking at two Dutch officers from across a Formica table. The man was tall and fair, the woman dark-haired and dark-skinned. Both of them studied Mia for some sign of...of a lie?

"Wait a minute. I didn't do anything," she blurted.

The female officer crossed her arms. "You were diving in the immediate area of *Neptune's Revenge* right before it exploded."

"So was the man who attacked me with a knife," she shot back.

"The man you *say* attacked you with a knife."

"A man with dark eyes and a blue hooded wetsuit and UltraFlow fins.... Wait a minute." Her heart thumped for a couple of beats before she managed to continue. "Why would I make something like that up?"

The male officer cut back in. "No one is saying you made anything up. We're just trying to gather the facts."

Facts. Like a ship blowing up practically in her face.

"What about the crew?" she blurted. God, please, don't let her have witnessed someone's death.

The officer shook his head. "Most of the crew was ashore. The two left on duty are in critical condition."

She hugged herself. *Please let them be all right. Please let them be all right.* "Where's Ryan?"

"Your friend, the police diver? The former Navy man?"

"Your friend, the expert in underwater explosives?" added the female officer, lifting her eyebrows.

Her friend, the expert in *what?*

Despite her shock, Mia found herself shooting to her feet. "My friend who saved my life!" she half shouted. Came within a hair of thumping a fist on the table as she said it, too. How could these cops possibly think Ryan was guilty of blowing up a ship? "He would never do anything like that!"

"No one is accusing your friend of anything," the man said, exchanging glances with his partner. Glances that said, *Yet. Not accusing yet.*

"This is ridiculous," she huffed. "He was with the dive group the entire time."

"Believe me, we are checking out his alibi."

The woman's look said, *Yours, too.*

Mia gaped at one police officer, then the other. Jesus, she wasn't just a witness to them. She was a suspect.

"But I didn't do anything! Ryan didn't do anything!"

"Why don't you just start at the beginning again?" the male officer suggested. His tone was even and patient, as if he had all evening to wait for her to trip over a lie.

Her throat went dry; her heart pounded. She ended up recounting the events of the day so many times, it felt like a week had gone by. Descending, following the diver in the distance, getting attacked. Barely making it to the surface before the ship exploded.

Her blood ran cold just thinking about it. The diver she'd tangled with had planted the bomb, but no one seemed to believe her.

"Can you describe the diver?"

"I told you! A man with dark eyes and UltraFlow fins."

"That's it?"

"He was wearing a hooded wetsuit and a dive mask!"

The officers looked unimpressed. "Nothing else?"

"I was too busy concentrating on other things!" she protested. "Like his knife."

The knife she could still picture flashing before her, even if she closed her eyes.

The interrogation went on and on, followed by a long hour in which she was left to sit, wonder, and plan calls to her aunt the lawyer. Then finally — finally! — the door opened and she was released to Hans and Lucky, who'd been waiting outside.

"I made a few calls," Hans said, patting her arm. At least he believed her. "They're letting you go."

"But they took my passport!"

Lucky nodded gravely. "You'll get it back. Believe me, we'll clear this up."

"Let's go." Hans pointed to the door.

She dug in her heels. "What about Ryan?"

"They're still questioning him."

"But he didn't do anything!"

Lucky cocked his head at her. "You know him, I think." It was a statement, not a question.

"You know him? How well?" Hans asked, sounding like a disapproving father.

She got stuck, trying to answer that one. Should she say, *Biblically? Sort of? Just a little bit?* Over the month they'd spent together, she felt like she'd gotten to know Ryan well. Really well. Not so much the facts, maybe, but as a person. He preferred listening to talking. Open air to confined spaces. She knew that he held doors open for little old ladies and tipped like a man who knew what it meant to work long hours on his feet. That he took a long time to get to sleep some nights, when he held her extra close. That he didn't laugh often, but when he did, it was like the sun coming out after a long, gray winter.

What else did a girl need to know about a guy to decide he was all right?

Other than the fact that he was a former Navy man trained in the use of underwater explosives and possibly other things, like killing giant squid with his bare hands. And that when push came to shove, she didn't mean as much to him as she'd let herself believe, because what he'd said about her to his friends. . .

She slammed on the brakes. Not going there. Not after a day like she'd had. And certainly not after a day in which Ryan had saved her so often, she was losing count.

She rocked on her heels and watched the clock tick. Lucky disappeared into a back office with another pair of officers, and she wondered if he was a suspect now, too.

At some point, a shadow appeared in the doorway from the inner offices, and it took her muddled mind a minute to process that it was Ryan standing there. Ryan, looking worn and tired and very, very pissed off.

It took her another long minute to realize the reason his arms were suddenly around her was that she'd practically tackled him into a hug that came out of she-wasn't-sure-where. Only that it felt good, getting him back again.

Whoa, Nelly. You haven't gotten anyone back again, the prudish part of her snapped. *You never wanted to see him again, remember?*

Right now, though, holding him felt right. Important, somehow. For a split second, she even felt his knees buckle before he steeled himself and went back to tough guy again.

He cleared his throat and jutted his chin to the door. "Let's get out of here."

"Yes, let's."

Stepping out of police headquarters was one thing. Deciding what to do next was another. The sun had just set, the streets were dark, and her head was spinning from a crazy afternoon.

"You can come to my house. Gerta and I will take care of you," Hans offered, standing in a way that made it clear the invitation was targeted at her, and her alone.

"I'm good," she insisted. "I need to get back home."

"Home?" Ryan's left eyebrow arched.

"To my boat."

Now both his eyebrows shot up. "Your boat?"

Okay, so maybe he wasn't the only one who'd held back some personal information.

"My boat." She nodded. *"Serendipity."*

He nodded slowly but his eyes were wide.

"It's a long story," she sighed. "Where are you going?"

Ryan looked at her, expressionless. Which, she knew, was a sure sign of trouble. The stronger Ryan felt about something, the less he'd let show it on the outside. She wanted to stomp a foot and wring the words out of him.

"Your dinghy is tied up at the town dock," Hans broke in. "And your boat is moored all the way across the bay. I won't let you do that alone."

"I've dinghied across the bay lots of times," she protested.

"Not after a day like today," Hans pointed out.

"I'll be fine," she said, hugging herself unconsciously, then immediately straightening. But damn it, in trying to avoid Hans' eyes, she made the mistake of latching on to Ryan's.

You don't have to go alone, his green eyes said.

Don't be ridiculous, she wanted to say. But the words wouldn't come. Her tongue flat-out refused to form them, and her lips were on strike, too.

"And anyway, it's nighttime," Hans went on.

Ryan didn't move or change expression in any way, but there they were, those unspoken words. *You don't have to go alone.*

"I go at night all the time," she tried, but she was wavering. Maybe Ryan was right. Maybe she didn't have to go alone. Maybe she didn't have to prove anything tonight. Maybe...

Please, his eyes said. Like he needed her to say yes. Desperately. Like it wasn't just about a trip home but about something much bigger than that. *Please. Please let me explain.*

A moped hummed past. Jazz music played from a bar somewhere down the street. Hans was still insisting on giving her a ride to his place. A waxing moon shone down from above, palms rustled overhead, and Ryan kept looking at her like *that,* saying, *Please.*

She'd nearly died that afternoon. Didn't she owe him this much?

"And anyway, don't worry," she finally managed, cutting Hans off. "I won't be alone."

Ryan caught his lower lip with his front teeth and held it, waiting.

"What?" Hans asked.

She jabbed a thumb toward Ryan, trying to play it cool. Like it was only a ride she was giving him and not a second chance.

"I won't be alone," she repeated. "He's coming with me."

A tiny smile played at the corners of Ryan's mouth, and if it had been a smile of triumph, she'd have shoved him away then and there. But his shoulders dipped at the same time, and she saw it for what it was: sheer relief.

"Now, wait a minute—" Hans started in exactly the same tone her dad might have used a couple of years ago, back before he finally accepted that his daughters were all grown up.

"Thanks, Hans. For everything," she said, giving him a quick hug. "I'll call you tomorrow, okay?"

Hans, she could tell, was glaring over her shoulder at Ryan. *One wrong move, young man, and I'll—*

She broke off the hug and steered Hans back toward the police building. "I wonder what's taking Lucky so long. Maybe you should check."

"Maybe I should," Hans said, though he barely budged.

"I'm exhausted," she said, because suddenly, she really was. "I need to get home. Thanks for everything, Hans. Tell Lucky the same."

She turned for the short walk to the waterfront, and Ryan fell into step at her side, so close and so comforting, she could have reached for his hand.

Her fingers warmed on something, and crap, she really had reached for his hand.

And double crap, her body leaned against his without her permission. Again.

Chapter Nine

Ryan got to wishing the town of Kralendijk was a bigger place, because he wouldn't have minded walking along like that a lot longer before getting to the dock. They hadn't done a lot of this sappy hand-in-hand thing back in New York, but damn, maybe they should have. The way their shoulders brushed, the way her fingers settled between his in a custom fit. It was kind of nice.

Okay, really nice.

Of course, he'd had a day of near-misses, and that had a way of doing weird things to a guy's head. Maybe tomorrow he'd think this was goofy. Maybe tomorrow he'd get his head screwed on right.

Or maybe tomorrow would feel as good as right now.

He'd been steaming back there in police headquarters. In New York, it would have been an hour, tops. But three hours of questioning? Small-town cops had way too much time on their hands. Small-town cops with big-world problems, like a terrorist bombing a boat in the harbor.

A terrorist, not him. He'd tried getting that point across again and again. *I'm just here for the diving... Saw Mia swim after some guy... A guy who took out a knife and...*

He closed his eyes and let her lead him through the dim streets. He didn't need to replay that scene. Didn't need to ruin the calm that settled over him the minute she took his hand.

So they'd taken his passport. The Dutch authorities here would check his record out, and by morning, everything would be fine. Yeah, everything would be fine. He should take his cue from the upbeat pastel colors of the colonial buildings they passed and make the most of his first trip outside the US in a couple of years, right?

"God, there he goes again," Mia muttered.

They were passing Rick's, a dockside, open-air bar where the dive boat had met its passengers that afternoon. Several members of the dive group were there, turned to a giant television screen where Stanley was showing his footage from the day.

"I was born in Holland, but I swear I'll die on Bonaire!" Hans said in the video clip.

"No, wait, let me fast-forward to the right place," Stanley broke in, leaning over his camera.

Ryan couldn't help pausing to watch the crazy day zip past in triple time. There was Mia, introducing the crew and passengers, looking happy as a lark until she'd realized he was there. He caught a glimpse of himself looking at her, and damn, why was his face that grim? What had he been thinking, giving her that cold stare?

Then the camera jumped over to dolphins and underwater views of the wreck and Brenda's cleavage and colorful fish until finally it surfaced and panned and... *Boom!*

Everybody watching flinched as if the ship were being blown up again. Mia shuddered then turned to speed-walk down the dock, and he followed.

Two figures leaned over the railing, watching the yellow lights of salvage boats working around *Neptune's Revenge*. It was listing badly but still afloat.

"A miracle they've managed to contain the oil..." said one.

"A miracle no one was killed," said the other.

The night was warm, but his blood ran cold. What if someone had been killed? What if it had been Mia?

Mia, he noticed, kept her eyes studiously away from the wreck. She knelt by a tangle of lines, slipped off her shoes, and maneuvered her way into a small rubber dinghy.

"Hop in."

The minute he got in, she pushed off from the dock, started the outboard with an expert yank on the starter cord, and took off, speeding into the night. There was about an inch of water in the bottom of the dinghy, but she didn't seem worried about that. She just picked up a cutoff milk container and started bailing.

"I got it." He took it from her hand and got to work. Scoop, splash. Scoop, splash. A cupful of water at a time, he got it back overboard where it belonged as they chugged onward.

The wind whipped Mia's hair as she looked forward, one hand steering the outboard, and damn if she didn't look as much at home as she'd been stepping into a subway car in New York.

"Why the purple outboard?" he asked, trying to melt the ice.

She shrugged. "My cousin Seth painted it to discourage thieves. He and—" She stopped abruptly and slapped her thigh. "Shit."

A word that could have applied to just about every part of his day, except maybe the moment she'd taken his hand.

"I was supposed to go food shopping today." She sighed. "My sister is going to kill me."

So her sister was on the boat. Good thing? Bad thing? He wasn't sure.

"I'm sure she'll cut you some slack after you tell her what happened."

Mia throttled down and looked at him so fiercely, he leaned back. The moon cast her face in black-and-white shadows as she snapped, "Do not tell her what happened. Do not!"

He blinked at the sudden outburst.

"She'll flip out," Mia said. "She already thinks diving is dangerous, and I get enough lectures from my parents about that. No way am I telling her what happened. No way. Got it?"

He put his hands up. "Got it, got it."

She nodded firmly and got back on course, throttling up again. He kept his mouth shut and watched the water ripple by, because Mia was Mia, and he'd do as he was told, if only to prove she could trust him.

If she ever would. But she'd trusted him this far, so that was something, right?

The outboard was only a little four-horsepower thing, so the dinghy wasn't setting any speed records, but from that close to the waterline and in the dark of the night, it still felt fast. A little like his whole day — zipping by in a blur of shadows and shapes.

"Where's your boat?"

"Over there."

"Where?"

"Way over there." She motioned into the darkness, marked only by dots of masthead lights.

"You didn't tell me about the boat," he murmured, trying not to let it sound like an accusation.

She shrugged. "You didn't you tell me about your job."

Yeah, he hadn't told her about a lot of things.

They chugged along in mutual silence, listening to the hum of the engine.

"We'd been planning it for a while, my sister and I." Mia started talking so quietly, he nearly missed her first words. "This trip." She let a second tick by before continuing. "I gave my job in Boston notice and everything." She paused again, and he had the sense that every sentence could have been a chapter in her life. "We were all set to fly to the Caribbean, but Seth and Julie — my cousin and his girlfriend, who were sailing the boat — got delayed bringing *Serendipity* across from Panama to here. So suddenly, we had another seven weeks to kill. A friend tipped me off about the short-term job in New York, so I took that to earn a little extra for this trip."

It was just like she'd said back then. *I'm only in New York short-term.*

Now it made sense: why she'd showed up out of nowhere at the pool where he swam laps, and why it'd been so hard to track her down after she left. Your average woman left New York for Philly or Chicago or some place like that, not a sailboat in the Caribbean.

"Is it your cousin's boat?"

She shook her head. "It's all of ours. My grandfather left it to all of us cousins."

He looked at her, wondering. When his grandfather died, he got a watch.

"Where are you sailing to next?" he asked, for lack of a more intelligent response.

"Grenada." She pointed like she had an internal compass and the place was just over there. "Three hundred ninety-five nautical miles."

He was still getting his jaw back into place when Mia jutted her chin toward the salvage operations, changing the subject. "Would that be the kind of thing you take care of?"

Ah, the long-avoided topic of his job.

He considered the scene. "We don't do salvage, but we'd secure the scene. Dive for evidence, check the hull. That kind of thing." And if they were lucky, preventing this kind of disaster.

She shook her head. "What's it like, diving in New York Harbor? I mean, diving there regularly. For work, not for fun."

"It's not like this, that's for sure." If New York had the crystal-clear water Bonaire did, everyone would want his job.

"So why do you do it?"

He'd heard the question a thousand times and had never really come up with an answer. Hadn't ever really tried. Either people got what it meant to be part of an elite squad doing important work, or they didn't. Mostly, they didn't.

He sure hoped Mia did. He searched for an answer. "I like how it's different, every day. I like the challenge."

"Like being in the Navy?"

He nodded. "Kind of like that." A lot like that, actually. Just closer to home, which was his whole point in leaving the Navy. Six years felt like enough time to be in a constant flux of shipping out or shipping in, and the police dive squad seemed like it would be a good fit. And it was. It was just that he was a little...not exactly burned out, because a good soldier didn't get burned out. He was just a bit...tired. Lately, he'd even been tempted to move on to Plan B: going civilian by taking an old Navy buddy up on the standing offer of a partnership in a dive salvage business down in the Florida Keys. Until Mia came along and put the spark back into things.

Spark. A sense of pride and purpose. Mia had helped him rediscover those things. And he didn't even realize it until she was gone.

She motored on in the darkness, and when she spoke again, her voice was hushed. "I'm sorry about those guys. That accident."

He sucked in a long breath. So she'd heard about it. Hell, all of the East Coast had heard about the freak accident that cost two of his squad their lives. A one-in-a-million combination of equipment failure, hellish currents, and an unlucky tangle with debris on the river bottom. No one could have foreseen it except some evil fate who'd chosen to concoct exactly that series of insurmountable obstacles in exactly that configuration.

He nodded. What else could he say?

Looked like he didn't need to say anything, because he could practically see the gears moving in her mind.

Work has been a little... all-consuming lately. I'd rather talk about other stuff.

Maybe it made sense to her now, what he'd told her back then.

"Mia, I wasn't trying to keep anything secret from you. I just... I just..." He couldn't quite get it out. *I just had enough of the questions eight million New Yorkers kept asking. I had enough of the press. I had enough of my mind replaying their funerals, again and again. Seeing their widows, their kids, all dressed in black. The tears. I just—*

"I get it," she said, cutting off that runaway train. She nodded into the darkness. "I get it."

There was more to say, lots more, and he knew he had to say it. Especially about what it had to do with that awful day when everything had gone wrong between them. About why his buddies had said what they did and why he didn't stop them.

It was his moment to finally, finally explain all that, and he knew it.

But a single point of light was gaining on them from behind, and he stopped to point it out.

"Somebody's passing. Can they see us?"

A cloud had passed in front of the moon, making the night darker still.

Mia glanced back and veered inshore, muttering something he couldn't catch. They were passing a beachside disco now, and the music was loud. Really loud.

"I said, grab the flashlight," she said, pointing to a pouch attached to the dinghy. "Shine it so they can see us."

He twisted the head of the flashlight and aimed the beam at the speeding motorboat.

"Don't worry, I'll just let them pass." Mia detoured a little farther right. "Plenty of space."

And there was, because they'd come to a section of the long, sprawling bay that was free of moorings. The area used for seaplane landings, if he remembered right.

The thing was, the motorboat detoured, too, and stayed right on their tail. His pulse ticked faster. What the hell?

"Hey!" Mia yelped, swerving left.

The motorboat swerved, too, bearing down on them fast. He could make out the aluminum bow, slicing through the water at a good twenty, maybe thirty knots. A hell of a lot faster than Mia's dinghy, puttering along at about three.

"Shine the light! Shine the light!" she yelled, throttling up and turning more.

"I am shining the light!"

The motorboat curved, intently following their wake.

God, a thousand-volt spotlight would come in handy right now to blind that suicidal driver before he did some real damage.

Then it clicked. The operator of that motorboat wasn't suicidal. More like homicidal. Ryan turned the light off.

"What are you doing?"

He didn't answer, except to yell as the oncoming powerboat thundered closer. "Turn! Turn!"

Mia yanked the outboard handle so far over, he thought the dinghy would flip.

Nrrrr-zoom! The powerboat roared past, inches away, slicing a curtain of water out of the sea and slapping it at them. Ryan ducked half a second too late to avoid getting drenched. When he looked up, spluttering, he barely made out two figures in the boat, motioning their way.

The motorboat sped ahead.

Mia threw it the finger and shouted. "Asshole!"

Apparently, she'd picked up a couple of bad habits in New York.

She'd barely gotten the dinghy back on course when the shadow of the motorboat lengthened, then shrank again. It wasn't carrying legal running lights, but Ryan could see its outline in the pale starlight. Side view; front view. It was turning around.

"Shit, they're coming back!" Mia yelled.

"Speed up!"

The outboard screamed in protest. "This is as fast as it goes!" She swerved toward the nearest cluster of boats, a good two hundred feet away.

"Faster!" he yelled, looking at the oncoming boat.

"Oh, God!" Mia leaned forward like a jockey urging on her mount.

"Turn! Turn!" he yelled.

She waited for what he was sure was a second too long before cutting aside, dodging the motorboat by the closest of margins. The dinghy surfed aside on the bow wave of the motorboat, its engine sputtering, nearly swamped.

Boom, boom, boom, boom, went the thumping bass from the raging party on shore. The noise covered up the roar of the motorboat and the choking pant of Mia's little outboard.

"Go! Go!"

Mia shot off again. One hundred feet to the closest boats, which seemed buttoned up for the night. Not a soul in sight to witness the crime.

The motorboat turned for another pass, and Ryan shook his head. He had no weapons, no defense. No way to keep Mia safe.

Think! Think!

Could he grab an oar and swing it? Throw it at the driver like a harpoon? Could he—

There was no time for any of that, though, because the motorboat was charging them again. Mia swung right, and in one blinding instant of that light bearing down on them, Ryan played it all out in his mind. The driver would anticipate this time and ram them, catching Mia's side. She'd be hit and thrown into the water. Never mind drowning, she'd be killed by the impact.

Every muscle in his body coiled.

Mia screamed, looking back — no, up — at the looming motorboat. He launched himself at her, trying to get it exactly right. Reaching for her, angling his body so it would shelter hers. To knock her far enough back that she'd be thrown clear. To—

There was a deafening roar, a slamming sensation, and then everything went black.

Chapter Ten

All Mia saw was the piercing light of the oncoming motorboat. All she heard was the murderous roar of the engine. Then something hit her — hard — and she went flying. There was a crash and a splash and great wall of water and a heaving pressure on her chest and—

Jesus, hadn't she had enough for one day?

Salt water flooded her nose and mouth. She flailed this way and that, seeking the surface, wherever it was. Swirling, swirling, and—

Air! She sucked in a lungful along with salt water and coughed so hard, it hurt. She paddled in no particular direction. The night was dark, the water darker still, and she couldn't tell which points of light were boats and which were stars for all the hair in her face.

She dipped her head back to clear it away. The drone of an engine sounded from the left — the motorboat rushing back for another pass at the dinghy, which floated at an odd angle a few strokes away.

"Ryan!" she screamed, turning in a desperate circle.

No sign of anything but the motorboat, which veered away from the dinghy and headed straight at her.

She barely had time to gulp a breath of air and dive before it was upon her. She jackknifed her head down, stuck her butt up, and kick-kick-kicked downward for her life.

The engine throbbed and the propeller sliced past, practically shaving the wake off her feet. She'd had enough of deep water for one day, but it was her only way out. Down, as deep as she could, then a couple of strokes sideways to come up in a different place.

When her desperate lungs forced her to surface again, she spluttered and coughed but didn't dare cry for Ryan again. Forcing herself to stay low, she breathed whatever air she could find a hair above the waterline. Where was the motorboat? Where was Ryan?

Vrrrroooom!

She spun around as the aluminum launch rushed by two boat-lengths away, ramming the dinghy. There was a dull scrape as the motorboat rode halfway up her poor inflatable, using sheer weight to drive it under.

Pffffsssssst! The dinghy ruptured with a violent hiss of air.

"Ryan!" She splashed in a circle, kicking upward to see better. God, where was he?

Any second now, the motorboat would be back for another pass. She could already hear the engine throttle down as it headed into a turn.

"Ry—"

She spotted a limp, dark lump in the water. She stroked toward it and snatched the back of his shirt. Bundling the fabric in her fist, she flipped him onto his back.

"Ryan!" She shook him then glanced up. The motorboat was coming back, slower this time. One man leaned over the bow, scanning the water with a light.

She grabbed Ryan by the collar and started kicking sideways toward an anchored sailboat. A big catamaran, judging by the high profile. If she could get him there, they could hide between the twin hulls.

She kicked while stroking with one arm, keeping the other tight in Ryan's shirt. He was quiet. Too quiet, too still. Knocked out? Injured? Worse?

Getting the most out of every stroke had never meant life-or-death before, and she threw everything into it. Kick, haul with her arm, kick again. Quietly, so the thugs in the boat wouldn't notice. Something was drawing their attention to the right, giving her a sliver of hope.

She gasped for air and kicked harder as a second light joined the first in seeking their prey.

Harder!

The motorboat coasted to a near stop as the lights stabbed the water here and there. The catamaran was only a couple of strokes away, but one of the lights was arcing slowly her way, reaching over the water like the beam of a lighthouse. Closer. Closer.

Harder! Kick!

She ducked between the twin hulls of the catamaran and hauled Ryan in an inch ahead of the beam. She held her breath and held perfectly still.

The light swept onward, passing over them.

Male voices murmured, barely carrying over the noise of the disco. She peeked and watched their silhouettes continuing past.

She ducked behind the catamaran hull again and grabbed Ryan's shoulders with both hands. Bent her head to his, listening for his breath. *Please, let there be a breath. Please, let there be—*

The faintest puff of air whispered over her ear, and she nearly cried in relief.

"Ryan?" she whispered, stroking his cheek.

He looked just the way he'd looked all those mornings when she'd woken up ahead of him in New York. Serene. Innocent. Boyish, even. Like he was dreaming of something really nice and never wanted to wake up.

But this wasn't a quiet morning in bed. This was nighttime in open water with a couple of thugs on a search-and-destroy mission, and she really, really needed him to wake up.

One of the men in the motorboat had to be the diver who'd attacked her that afternoon. The bomber. And now he was back to eliminate her, the witness. God, how had she gotten into this mess? Somehow, the men had figured out which diver she was, which wouldn't have been too difficult, thanks to that pink and purple wetsuit of hers. They must have followed her to the police station and eventually shadowed her to the dinghy.

It wouldn't have been hard to follow a lone dinghy through the anchorage and strike when the time was just right.

She peeked again. It was impossible to identify either of the men in the motorboat, just as it had been impossible to identify the diver, but every nerve in her body said that had to be him.

One of the men muttered at the other, and they circled the area again. The dinghy was a useless lump held afloat by the last chamber of air that hadn't been punctured. Her cousins were going to kill her when they heard about the dinghy. Her sister was going to kill her. Her—

She held the thought there, because none of that mattered if she didn't get out of this mess alive.

The launch powered up and sped away, apparently satisfied with their night's work, and Mia watched it go. One obstacle down. How many yet to overcome?

She'd just started maneuvering Ryan over to the swim platform on one of the catamaran's twin sterns when he sputtered and jerked.

"Ryan!"

He mumbled and twisted his head left and right, looking past her as he floundered in the water. "Mia?"

She gave him a little shake. "Here. Right here. God, are you all right?"

"Are you all right?" he echoed, focusing on her face. He reached out and grabbed her shoulder like *she* was the one needing rescuing.

She went warm all over, seeing Ryan look at her like that. Like nothing mattered but her. Like he *needed* her to be all right.

"I'm good. All good. What about you? Wait, get over this way."

She pulled him toward the swim platform and he gave in, going a little floppy again.

"Hold on to this," she said, guiding his hand to the ladder submerged in the water. "Are you really okay?" She started patting him down one side of his body and up the other. Her fingers traced his ribs, then his shoulders, and then his head.

When she touched his left arm, he winced a little then shook his head, clearing the water out of one ear.

"Are they gone?"

"Yeah." She gulped, nodding in the direction the motor-boat had gone. "They're gone."

He heaved a great breath. "Christ, Mia..."

She got caught between an inhale and an exhale, knowing just what he meant. "Yeah. God, that was..."

She gave up on words and wrapped her arms around him instead, squeezing him as close as she could. Not the easiest operation, what with the swim ladder in one hand, but nothing would stop her now. Nothing. For a minute, they breathed right into each other's skin. A minute in which it didn't matter that they were in the middle of nowhere in the middle of the night.

Then a tiny ripple of water splashed the catamaran, and it mattered again. When Ryan pulled away, part of her wailed inside.

"You want to know the bright side?" She forced herself to say, just to keep her cool.

"There's a bright side to being marooned in the water at night?"

She nodded. "There's a bright side to everything, dummy. You just have to look for it."

He looked at her like she was nuts, then made a show of looking right, left, up, and down. "Uh, the moon is giving us some light?"

"No. The police took our passports, so those are nice and safe."

He laughed out loud, and it did her good to hear that, to see his smile.

"And dry."

"Drier than us, at least."

He looked at her like he was going to say something, but he didn't say anything at all. Just looked and looked until she wanted to tap him on the side of the head to tip the words out.

"Drier than us," he agreed at last, shooting her a little smile. Then he flipped a switch and went back to serious again. All cop. All soldier. All Ryan, for lack of a better word.

"Where's your sailboat?" he asked, scanning the anchorage.

She pointed. "All the way at the far side. We're about halfway there. About another mile to go."

He muttered something, then took a long, steadying breath. Under normal circumstances, neither of them would bat an eye at that distance, but tonight...

She looked around. Tonight, she wouldn't be above borrowing someone's dinghy, but there was nothing in sight. It was swim or nothing.

"Easy," he lied, obviously trying to bolster her nerves.

"Easy," she lied back, trying to bolster his. "We did three times that in a single workout in New York."

"Right," he murmured.

"Right."

Neither of them moved for a long time.

"If it gets to be too much, we can always detour to shore," she tried.

"Sure." He sounded about as enthusiastic about it as she did.

"Right. Ready, Eddie?"

His lips quirked at the line she'd used to challenge him back in the pool.

She waited for him to echo with his standard reply. *Born ready.*

But he didn't. He went all serious again, intent on something on her face. He leaned closer and pulled lightly at the same time, making her wonder what he was going to brush off her skin. A piece of seaweed? Her hair?

But he didn't brush. Didn't move a hand. He only moved his lips, pressing them against hers in a kiss very much like their very first one, back in New York. A kiss that barely had any motion to it but still managed to roll fireballs through her nerves.

That short, sweet kiss lasted forever — the best kind of forever — in her mind. They could have been in her favorite brunch place in Brooklyn, kissing for the first time, or Central Park, or on the stoop outside her apartment. It didn't matter where or when or why. It only mattered that he was there.

Then Ryan let go and nodded, like he was satisfied he'd gotten it right. Which he absolutely, positively had, because every panicked nerve in her body had settled down and was now happily humming along.

"Born ready," he murmured and nodded across the bay.

Chapter Eleven

Just like in the pool, Ryan told himself, stroking along through the water at Mia's side. Right arm, left arm, kick-kick-kick, just like in the pool. Making his body long and lean, rolling with every stroke to cut through the water like a fish.

His right arm twinged a little, reminding him that this was not in the least bit like the pool because it was goddamn dark, above and below, and the water was as endless as the night sky. And if the current set in any time now, they'd be royally screwed.

But other than that...just like the pool, right?

He'd done this kind of swim in the Navy, so he sure as hell could do it again. And even nighttime in Bonaire beat noon in the East River, so he'd manage just fine.

Fine. Perfectly fine. He repeated the words like a mantra with every stroke.

He was running on empty, and he knew it, but that kiss worked as fuel. A fringe benefit he hadn't been thinking about when he did it, because the kiss kind of just happened, just...just because. He played it over and over in his mind. How good it felt. How right. For Mia, too. He replayed her tiny gasp of surprise at the start and her little moan when they'd broken apart. The way her hands tightened around his back like she never wanted to let go. The way he'd clutched her, like *he* never wanted *her* to let go.

When she'd left him in New York, it had taken three weeks to realize how bad he had it for her. But now... Crap, he didn't just have it bad, he was in deep. In more ways than one.

Focus, man!

Mia was getting ahead; he needed to keep his head in the game. She swam like she knew exactly where she was going, which was a damn good thing, because he had no idea. No idea what they'd do when they got to her boat, or what they'd do after that, or after whatever came next.

But they'd cross those bridges when they came to them. Eventually. Right now, he'd better concentrate on catching up.

Her leg bumped his, and he got a little rush, like he always did when she touched him. A minute later, she did it again, but it was more of a kick. He sputtered to a stop to give her a little space.

He looked up, and it struck him that she was a full length ahead. Too far away to have kicked him.

An itchy, crawling feeling worked its way down his spine. If Mia hadn't brushed up against him, then...

"Stop!" he called. He treaded water with the smallest movements possible. "Stop!"

Mia splashed to a stop, and he winced, looking around for the fin he was certain must be cutting through the water.

He looked left. No fin.

Jerked his head right. No fin.

Looked straight down into the inky water. Couldn't see a damn thing.

"What?" Mia called. "Why did you sto—"

A sleek form cut through the water between them, barely making a splash. It was too dark to make out any detail, but it was big. Plenty big. Phosphorescence sparkled in its wake, which might have been kind of cool if it weren't for the shark-attack music playing in the back of his mind.

"Oh my God!" Mia whispered, following the shape with her eyes.

He swam over to her side and went back-to-back with her. "You see anything?"

Her voice wavered when she answered. "It went that way."

He couldn't tell which way *that way* was, but it didn't sound good.

"Maybe we should swim to shore," Mia tried. "Or climb out on the nearest boat."

He looked. Shore was a long way away, and the nearest boat wasn't all that near.

"Oh!" Mia jolted half a second after he did. "Did you feel that, too?"

Yeah, he'd felt it. Wished he could feel his dive knife strapped to his calf where he kept it whenever he dove in open water. Only he hadn't been planning on going swimming tonight, so no knife. No weapon, no light.

"Probably just a fish," he lied.

"Right," Mia whispered. "A fish."

And then it was back, sweeping right past them, brushing along his shoulder and hers, and he punched at the water. They said sharks were sensitive around the snout, but where the hell was the snout? He couldn't see a thing.

"Wait! Look!" Mia grabbed his arm.

Phosphorescence flashed again, all along the sleek back disappearing into the water, illuminating a fin and, a second later, a tail.

He blinked as it disappeared in the water. Not the vertical tail of a shark, but the horizontal tail of—

"A dolphin!" Mia squeaked. "Dolphins!"

A second splash followed the first, and he saw it then, too. The perfectly round blowhole on its head, the crooked smile of a mouth. Two — no, three dolphins were running laps around them. He could hear them clicking in dolphin Morse code.

"Dolphins," he managed, then laughed out loud.

"Dolphins," Mia cried, spinning in a slow circle to watch them glide by.

They watched in stunned silence for a minute, and he willed his heart rate to settle down.

"Want to give us a ride to *Serendipity*, Flipper?" Mia called.

Flipper didn't answer, but that was okay. As long as it was Flipper and not Jaws, he wouldn't complain.

"Bye, Flipper." Mia gave a little wave as the phosphorescence moved away and faded.

He let out a slow breath. "Bye-bye, Flipper. Just don't give me a heart attack next time, please."

Mia chuckled, and that wave of tickling heat rolled through him again. There she went again, finding the bright side in everything. Keeping her nerve when it counted most. Looking at him like maybe there was a bright side in him too, and all she had to do was look hard enough.

"Not far now," she murmured after another quiet second ticked by.

And just like that, she was off again.

He could finally make out what she was aiming for: three boxy yellow lights, topped by a white one higher up. Every time he raised his head up high enough to look, they drew a little closer until the boxes became the windows of a cabin. A cozy cabin, from the look of it, on a cozy little boat.

A couple more strokes and he had the rung of a swim ladder tight in his hand. Mia was there already, looking back the way they'd come with big eyes that couldn't quite believe it was over. Then she dipped her head back to get the hair away from her face just like she did at the pool in that move that was guaranteed to turn a dozen heads, and clambered up the ladder, giving him a perfect view of her perfect ass.

Not that he was thinking about *that* at a time like *this*. Not in the least.

He came up behind her, dripping all over the deck.

Mia hopped from the aft deck into the cockpit and called inside. "Meredith?"

Right, the sister. He looked down at his dripping shorts, the shirt clinging to his chest. He looked like a drowned rat.

"Mia? Is that you?" A voice a little higher than Mia's called, and her sister appeared in the companionway.

"Yeah, it's me," Mia said, grabbing a towel off the lifelines strung around the cockpit.

"Oh my God, are you all right?" Meredith jumped out and caught her sister in a huge hug.

Ryan felt like he ought to look away, but he couldn't quite do it. The little Mia had ever told him about her sister didn't make it sound like they were particularly close, but that hug said differently. That hug said they were family.

It showed, and not just in the hug. They looked a lot alike. The same narrow chin, the same slender face. The same build, if he took away Mia's swimmer's shoulders. Meredith's long hair was darker than Mia's but just as straight, and she had that same could-be-nobody, could-be-a-secret-superstar kind of poise that kept a guy guessing every time he peeked.

"Why are you all wet?" Meredith asked, breaking off the hug. She kept one hand on Mia's shoulder exactly like a mom would do. The caring older sister, through and through.

"Wait, where's the dinghy?"

Mia looked at her feet. "You don't want to know."

Meredith's right eyebrow arched as she glanced his way, a little wary. "And who is this?"

Mia shook her head and murmured, "You *really* don't want to know."

He sighed a little inside. So they were back to that, were they?

"Ryan Hayes," he said, leaning in to shake Meredith's hand.

"Nice to meet you, Ry—" she started, before her eyebrows shot up. She turned to Mia. "*That* Ryan?"

He winced, because Meredith's tone didn't imply oh-my-God-is-this-that-sweet-Ryan-you-told-me-about? It certainly didn't say, Ryan-who-made-your-toes-curl-Ryan? More like Ryan-rat-bastard-Ryan-who-betrayed-you-Ryan? Ryan-whose-nuts-you'd-like-to-put-in-a-vise-Ryan?

Mia sighed a heavy sigh. "That Ryan."

Meredith looked at him, cocking her head. It looked like she was reserving judgment — for the time being, at least. "Well, welcome aboard, Ryan," she said, then added a quieter, "I think."

God, it had been a long day. And it sure looked like it might be a long night.

"We have to get moving," Mia said, uncoiling the lines by a winch on the starboard side.

"Going? Where?" Meredith protested.

"It's a long story."

Meredith looked at him to embellish, but he kept his mouth shut. Mia told him not to say anything about the dive that day, right? And anyway, it was bad enough that Mia was in danger. The more they told Meredith, the more she'd be dragged into the mess, too. Okay, she was already dragged in, but still. He crossed his arms, sealed his lips, and became the audience to a two-woman show.

"It's night. It's dark." Meredith gestured wildly. "We can't go anywhere right now!"

"We have to go," Mia grunted, moving to the other side.

"The engine's out. You know that. Mia, what's going on?"

Mia stopped and slumped over the winch. God, she looked tired. Really tired. "I saw the man who bombed that ship today. *Neptune's Revenge*."

"You what?"

Mia barely moved, though he sensed a tiny tremble. He nearly went to her side, but Meredith got there first, reaching a hand to Mia's shoulder in one of those sister-sister moments a guy had no business barging in on.

"Don't worry. My friend Celeste said they had the suspects in custody," Meredith said.

Mia let out a bitter snort. "They had *us* in custody."

"They what?" Meredith hit a high note.

Mia waved her hand like that wasn't the point. "Listen, we have to get out of here. Whoever bombed that boat is after us now. And if they figure out I'm on *Serendipity*... God, Mer, they could come after us here. They could come after the boat!"

Ryan cocked his head at her. Someone had tried to kill her twice that day and she was worried about a boat?

"*Serendipity?*" Meredith wrung her hands and breathed the name like it was holy or something.

"Yeah, *Serendipity*. We have to move in case they come looking."

"Move where?"

Mia straightened and looked north, along the dark coast-line. "You know that anchorage we stopped at one day? The one tucked under a cliff? Wilhelm's Baai?"

"The one surrounded by reefs?"

"Reefs we made it through once before."

"At noon, with the sun lighting up the pass."

"We have the way points. There's an obelisk there, too. The one you line up with the tree to run the pass."

"Are you crazy?"

He was wondering the same thing.

"Do you have a better idea?"

"Yes! We go to the police." Meredith's anxious fingers twisted the hem of her white shirt.

Mia shook her head. "We were just there. They won't help. Look, we can do this, okay?" Her voice had that forced kind of certainty to it. "We can do this, Mer. We have to."

Okay, maybe it was time to step in.

"Mia, the boat's not worth risking your life."

She turned to him, and even in the moonlight, he could see her face go red. "My grandfather sailed this boat for thirty years and never hurt it!"

Hurt it, she said. Like it was a living, breathing thing and not an inanimate object.

Mia rushed on. "My cousins sailed it all the way from the US to the Caribbean and never damaged it."

"They did come close, though," Meredith murmured.

Mia ignored her, gathering steam. "Seth and Julie sailed it all the way here, against the wind!" She jabbed a finger at his chest. "All the way here and nothing ever happened. I am not letting anything happen to this boat!"

He looked to Meredith for support, but she just nodded at Mia and said, "You're right."

Great. He had not one but two stubbornly suicidal sailor chicks on his hands.

A dull buzzing noise sounded in the distance, and they all looked up. A low white light crept slowly across the bay. No, two lights, shining from a small motorboat, swinging to inspect one boat after another. Searching.

The boat was a good mile away and moving slowly, but that didn't stop his heart from thumping against his chest. If that was who he thought it might be, it was only a question of time before they honed in on *Serendipity.*

"Um... Anchors aweigh?" He looked at Mia.

She gave him a firm nod. "Anchors aweigh."

Chapter Twelve

Ryan watched the sisters jump into action. For a couple of stubbornly suicidal sailors, they sure seemed to know what they were doing.

"What can I do?" he asked.

Mia pointed to the corner of the cockpit. "Sit. We got this. You keep an eye on that motorboat."

He sat and steamed. *Sit?* You didn't tell an officer of the NYPD to sit!

Of course, she just had. And that was Mia. She'd had him from day one with that combination of tough and capable, humble and sweet. So he sat, damn it. What choice did he have?

Mia and Meredith moved around the deck like a couple of long-legged gazelles, preparing to get underway.

"Backup mooring line off," Mia said, tossing a coiled line into the cockpit.

"Wheel unlocked," Meredith replied.

They were going through a checklist, he realized. One they had down pat. What was it Mia had said about her grandfather and thirty years?

"Mainsheet free," Meredith called softly.

Mia stood by the mast and sniffed the wind like an old sea dog. Then she started hauling on a halyard, hoisting the mainsail up in creaky stages.

He jerked his head toward the motorboat, but the sound hadn't seemed to carry. Clouds still obscured the moon, so the white sail wasn't reflecting much light. Good. He glanced back at the sisters scurrying around the little sailboat.

From the looks of it, they'd spent a lot of time on the boat from the time they could walk. Maybe even before. Even Meredith, with her wary, cautious air became a different person as she moved expertly around the boat. She secured a little inflatable kayak on deck, then stood by the wheel with the mainsheet in her hand.

"Ready?" Mia called.

The sisters looked at each other for a long minute.

"Ready," Meredith whispered.

Mia slipped one end of the mooring line free, hauled it in, and raised a fist in some kind of signal.

"Underway," Meredith murmured, tightening the mainsheet.

A gentle southeast breeze filled the sail and just like that, they were ghosting away. No engine, no shouting, no fuss.

Ryan nodded. Even the oldest, crankiest Navy man would heartily approve of this crew. The tidy lines, the clean decks, the perfect teamwork. Everything but the apparent lack of hierarchy, because just when he'd decided Mia was the captain, Meredith would spin the wheel and scan the water like she was the one in charge. And somehow it worked. Seamlessly.

"Nav lights?" Meredith asked as Mia headed below to check the chart.

Mia gave her a grim shake of the head. "No nav lights. Course north by northwest."

"North by northwest," Meredith echoed, glancing down at the illuminated compass in front of the wheel. She steered with small, easy movements as her eyes flicked from the compass to the horizon and back.

If he'd given the two sisters a couple of beards and striped shirts, they'd be ready to star in an action movie — the kind with swords and buccaneers. He could imagine Mia perfectly, swinging on a line and slashing her way into the fray. Meredith, well, she'd be the quiet, dependable one at the wheel. The subtle differences between the two sisters were becoming clearer to him now. Mia had a lot of tomboy in her quick, assured movements, while Meredith was more cautious, like she'd learned a few life lessons the hard way. He had to wonder just what had done that to her.

In any case, they were kind of endearing, both of them, each in her own way.

"Why no motor?" he whispered to Meredith.

"A spring in the oil pump rusted. The new one I ordered hasn't arrived yet," she said, twisting to glance astern.

A woman who knew diesel engines. He nodded like he'd known that all along. Meredith was full of surprises. Just like Mia, who'd gotten the jib unfurled and the sheets trimmed, and then come to him to slide a gentle hand up his arm.

"You okay?"

"Okay," he murmured, wondering if he'd ever get a chance to make things right between them again.

She looked deep, deeper, nine-fathoms-deep into his eyes, searching for some truth. He hoped to hell it was there.

"How's the depth here?" Meredith asked, breaking the hush.

Mia shook her head like she'd been far away in her thoughts. "We're clear for the next couple of miles. Just stay well off the coast."

"No sign of that boat?"

All three of them twisted to look back. It was still there but hadn't detected their departure. At least not yet.

Mia took a deep breath and turned to her sister. "What else did you hear about the sabotaged ship?"

"Well, Celeste said—"

"Who's Celeste?" he asked.

"A friend of mine," Meredith said. "She's a local doctor I met at the clinic."

He cocked his head.

"Meredith's a doctor," Mia explained, and he could hear the pride in her voice. "She's been volunteering at the clinic."

Meredith waved a hand in a gesture so like Mia's when she wanted to divert attention from herself. "Except for the couple of years that she studied in Holland, Celeste has always lived here. She knows everyone."

"So what did she say?"

"She said her cousin who works next door to the police station told her they had suspects in custody."

"Yeah," Mia said glumly. "Us."

Meredith shook her head and went on, "Celeste said her other cousin the hairdresser said—"

"The hairdresser?" Ryan blurted.

"Hey, who's always the first to catch local gossip?"

He had to give her that one.

"Celeste's cousin the hairdresser said everyone suspects those developers."

His ears perked up. "What developers?"

"That big international company that's been petitioning to build a new hotel."

"Why would a hotel developer bomb environmental activists?" he asked, watching the low-lying coastline slide past as *Serendipity* picked up speed. Other than a few clusters of houses and the main town of Kralendijk, the island looked relatively undeveloped. An arid, windswept island, scoured by the trade winds. Did they really need more development here?

"The hotel isn't the issue. It's the pontoon they want to build."

"Pontoon?"

"Like a floating luxury hotel, right on the reef," Mia explained. "Right on some of the best diving in the world, and on a fragile reef. *Neptune's Revenge* was here to bring attention to that plan."

"Well, they brought attention to it, all right," he muttered. "But would the developers really be that stupid to bomb them when they'd be the first suspects?"

"Except we're the first suspects, remember?" Mia said. "Or rather, you, Officer Hayes of the...bomb squad, was it?"

"Dive squad," he murmured, forcing himself to meet her eyes. "The underwater explosives stuff was with the Navy."

If Meredith looked impressed, Mia sure wasn't.

I'll tell you everything, Mia, he wanted to say. *Just ask, and I'll start from the beginning and tell it to you right to the end.*

But she didn't ask, so he didn't say. Just held on to her eyes and willed her to believe.

Meredith looked at Mia, then him, then back at Mia, and finally plowed on. "It doesn't have to be the developer. It could be someone with a stake in the company or a competitor who could step in if that developer couldn't build. Really, it could be anyone."

"Not anyone," Mia growled. "A guy with dark eyes and a blue wetsuit and UltraFlow fins."

Meredith's eyebrow shot up, but Ryan just nodded. Leave it to Mia to notice the brand of the guy's dive gear.

"Not much to go on," Meredith said.

They all fell into silence, each of them shooting covert glances over their shoulders. Mia made constant adjustments to the lines, harnessing every breath of the light sea breeze.

Ryan closed his eyes and let the wind comb his hair. His salty skin itched, but that wind was fresh and invigorating, and thank goodness for that, because when things eventually slowed down tonight, his body was going to crash and crash hard.

A quiet hour ticked past as they inched closer and closer to escape.

"Clearing the cape," Meredith murmured.

"Not far now," Mia whispered, almost to herself. "This is the tricky part."

As *Serendipity* nosed around the corner of the bay, the lights of town winked out of sight, one by one. Ryan wasn't the only one who sighed a little in relief. The boat heeled a couple of degrees harder as they angled into the wind, and the gentle rocking motion became a lively romp. He eyed the dark coastline ahead. Where exactly were they headed?

"You can't see it until you're on top of it," Mia murmured, seeing him peer ahead. "It's just a tiny cut in the coast, but once you're in, it opens up to a little bay. No obstructions."

"Once you're in, that is," Meredith muttered. "The pass, on the other hand..."

Mia nodded. "The pass is a little narrow."

"And hard on the wind." Meredith pointed out.

And we have no working engine to help us power through it, he read in the nervous glances they exchanged.

Mia didn't comment. She just went below and eyed the chart. He peeked over her shoulder to see for himself and, Christ, that pass was narrow. When he looked up to match the chart with the view, he heard the murmur of waves breaking over a reef.

"Okay, we're almost there."

He watched Mia fiddle with the GPS, calling up the way points they had marked on their previous trip in — points that would guide them to safety like Hansel and Gretel's trail of crumbs. Or better than a trail of crumbs, he hoped. But damn, the pass looked narrow, a tiny cut between razor-sharp reefs. One degree off and they'd be sunk — literally.

"You don't have a pair of night vision goggles, do you?" he tried.

Both sisters laughed dryly.

Right. This wasn't the Navy or the NYPD. It wasn't a fancy yacht either, just a sturdy little workhorse that had been lovingly kept up over the years. He could see it in the woodwork, in the polish of the brass. Serendipity was what you might call a good old boat, low on electronic gizmos but high in old-fashioned faith in Lady Luck. If he ever met the cousin who'd brought this boat all the way down from New England, he'd shake his hand — or her hand, because it sounded like Mia and Meredith had a whole pack of Amazonian relatives just as capable of handling this boat as they.

Sailing blind through a reef, he didn't like. But the crew — these sailors, this family — he liked. Figured he'd have liked the grandfather, too.

"I can keep lookout on the bow," he offered.

She shook her head. "I'm on the bow. You're watching the GPS."

He blinked, slowly processing the fact that he had just been given an order. His gut rolled that one back and forth for a second before he nodded. It was her boat, after all.

She pointed at the display and briefed him on the data points they had saved from their last time through.

"Nothing to it," he nodded.

"Right," she muttered and disappeared out onto the deck.

Seconds ticked by, then ponderous minutes, as the icon on the GPS inched closer to the dark line of reefs. Closer. Closer...

"See the obelisk?" Mia called from the bow.

He couldn't see a goddamn thing.

"Got it," Meredith replied in a tight voice. "There's the pass. Our angle's no good, though. We'll have to try on the next tack."

Try. The operative word in that sentence. Not good.

He looked at the chart. The pass was narrow enough as it was — eye-of-the-needle narrow — and with the wind on the nose, they were going to have to zigzag in. A tricky proposition even by day. Suicidal by night.

The muted sound of foam grew louder.

"How much closer, Mia?" Meredith called anxiously.

"Just a little more... a little more..."

"Mia, the reef's right there!"

"Just a little more... ready... ready... Now! Now! Come about!"

Meredith spun the wheel hard, and the boat leaned over the other way. The boom came over with a dull thump just as Mia came running back to help haul in the sheets. The cacophony of sound and motion settled into an edgy kind of quiet a minute later, when Mia scampered back to the bow to keep lookout again.

They repeated the nerve-racking maneuver three times: edging right up to the reef before jerking away, inching closer to the pass every time. He kept a finger on the thin line of the pass on the chart and called out depth and bearings. The swishing sound of waves smashing into the reef became a roar from all sides.

"Straighten up! Straighten up! Ten degrees to port!" Mia cried from the bow.

He waited for the crunch of hull against reef.

"Ten degrees to port," Meredith echoed in a shaky voice.

The reef was thundering now, swallowing them up, the boat bouncing in the turbulent waters of the narrow pass. He gripped the chart table with both hands and watched the depth-sounder plunge. "Thirty feet...twenty..." he called out. "Fifteen..."

Serendipity's keel was five feet deep, and the chart showed ten feet at low tide. Plenty of water — theoretically.

"Back five!" Mia called.

The stern lurched sideways with an errant wave. It was like stumbling into a boxing ring where two prizefighters — the ocean and the reef — were duking it out, and all *Serendipity* could do was duck the punches — or try.

"Mia!" Meredith yelped.

He didn't hear Mia's answer because the fight escalated until they were in a deafening arena. The waves rushed. The rigging creaked. The wind moaned and—

Shhhhmmm. From one moment to the next, the noise faded to a murmur astern. *Serendipity* was through the pass and into the sheltered bay.

"I see the mooring!" Mia called with a heaven-be-praised note in her voice.

The boat glided forward, and he popped up onto the deck just in time to see Mia catch a white mooring ball. The boat glided to a graceful stop as Meredith let the sheets loose, and that was it. They were in.

He sat down hard, heart still pumping in double time.

Chapter Thirteen

Mia clutched the mooring line so tightly, it dug into her palms. Long after she looped it around a cleat in a double figure eight, she kept right on clutching, because they had made it. *Serendipity* was safe.

She tipped her head back, found Orion in the sky, and muttered a little thank you to whatever god or ghosts had let them squeeze into that tiny, sheltered bay. Pretending her heart wasn't beating halfway out of her chest, she examined the bay as if she sailed through narrow passes with no engine as backup in the middle of the night all the time.

God, they'd done it. They really had.

The bay was theirs, and theirs alone. A high ridge of land curved around that little scoop of water, protecting *Serendipity* from the wind, the waves, and from the view of casual passersby.

She'd barely dropped the mainsail and jumped into the cockpit when her sister caught her in a hug.

"We did it," Meredith murmured. There wasn't a trace of triumph in her voice, only relief.

"Yeah, we did it."

The two of them stood there, hanging on to each other like they hadn't done since first or second grade, and it struck her that this was what her granddad meant by getting back in touch. Not just with the big, wide world, but with each other. Ever since college, they'd taken two separate paths, but now... It was like coming home after a long, long time away.

Home. *Serendipity.* She sniffed a little into her sister's shoulder.

"Grandpa would be proud," Meredith whispered. Her eyes shone when she pulled back.

Mia nodded. Yeah, he would be. "Of both of us." That part was important to say, because Meredith, for all her accomplishments, still needed every reminder she could get.

Then Mia remembered it wasn't just her and her sister standing there. Ryan stood quietly to one side, looking a little bashful and a lot curious, like a merman studying human ways.

A very buff, very quiet merman with emerald eyes that said, *Mortal sailor, you have done well.*

Time jumped a little, and suddenly she was wrapped around him in a hug that had no beginning and no end. And for the first time since the craziness of the day started, eons ago, she felt like maybe, just maybe, things would be all right. Which just went to show how muddled her mind was, because things were absolutely, positively, not all right.

Something shifted by her elbow, and she drew reluctantly back from Poseidon — er, Ryan — to find her sister lowering the inflatable kayak over the side.

"What are you doing?"

Meredith walked the kayak to the stern. "I'm going ashore."

"You're what?" she and Ryan cried at the same time.

Meredith tied the kayak off and headed to the cabin, stuffing a few things in a backpack. "The boat is safe here, and you need to rest. But I need to find out what's going on."

Mia blinked. Her sister had just undergone one of those superwoman transformations she managed from time to time, going from uncertain, second-guessing Meredith to cool-calm-and-collected Meredith, the way she did when she headed out to work. Typical Meredith: a woman who could handle anything — blood and guts, crying babies, anything but the mess of bad memories in her mind.

"I'll call Celeste," Meredith started, already dialing, "and ask her to pick me up. She'll know what to do, who to go to." She held up a hand and spoke into the phone. "Hello, Celeste? It's Meredith..."

Mia glanced toward shore. It wasn't very far, and there was a narrow track up the bluff they'd been up last time they were here. She could barely think straight. Maybe Meredith was right. But if her sister left now...

She glanced at Ryan. Maybe he was thinking along the same lines, because the minute she looked up, he looked away. A few renegade nerve endings tingled, but the rest just lurched. If Meredith left, the two of them would be alone together, and sooner or later, they'd have to shovel away the dirt pile she'd allowed to build up between them. God, was she really ready to face that?

"Come on, hop in." Meredith strapped on her backpack and motioned to the kayak.

Mia blinked. *She* was supposed to be the one who could come to snap decisions while her sister wavered between a thousand pros and cons.

"Paddle me to shore, then paddle back so you have the kayak, just in case," Meredith said.

Which made sense, given that the dinghy had been sunk by criminals intent on killing her a couple of hours ago.

Suddenly Mia's whole body felt like lead. God, she was tired. Really, really tired.

"I'll go," Ryan said, putting a hand on her arm.

She closed her eyes, feeling so, so close to saying yes. But getting her sister to land was her job. After all, she was the one who had gotten them into this mess. She'd better be the one getting them out, no matter how tempting it was to look for a hero to do the dirty work.

"I got it," she said.

"You sure?"

The same question she asked her sister once they'd paddled ashore and stood on firm ground once again. "You sure about this, Mer?"

Meredith nodded. "I got this, and Celeste will help. But what about you? Are you sure?" She tilted her head toward the boat and Ryan, who stood sentinel at the stern as he had from the second they'd pushed off.

"I'm not sure of anything right now," Mia sighed, trying not to look his way.

Meredith studied her. "I'm worried about you."

"I'm worried about the boat."

"The boat will be fine. But you've been through a lot."

Mia nearly laughed, because her sister didn't know the half of it. "I'll be fine."

"I suppose you do have a bodyguard," Meredith said with a sly smile. "A pretty formidable one, too."

She sighed, not quite sure if Ryan was a problem or a solution.

"Plus, I figure you guys can use a little space," Meredith added.

"Space?" Things had seemed clearer when Tall, Dark, and Hunksome was a thousand miles away and much, much easier to hate.

"He is a cop, right?"

"A cop out of his jurisdiction by about five thousand miles."

"You'll figure it out," Meredith whispered, catching her in a goodbye hug.

Mia wondered whether her sister meant she'd figure out what to do about the bad guys after her, or what to do with the good guy she wasn't sure she was ready to face. But either way, she allowed herself a minute of comfort, too. This was the closest they'd gotten to a sisterly heart-to-heart in a long time, and it felt good.

"Get some sleep," Meredith said. "I'll call you in the morning."

And just like that, her sister was off, up the hill and out of sight, leaving Mia blinking back an out-of-the-blue wave of tears and clutching the kayak paddle like it was an anchor or compass or something — anything — that would get her out of this mess.

Chapter Fourteen

Ryan watched Mia paddle back the same way he'd watched her paddle to shore: like a hawk, because all she needed now was another stroke of crap luck, like the inflatable kayak popping a hole or a submarine attack or God knows what other challenge might crop up in her day.

And man, it had been a hell of a day.

She'd hugged her sister goodbye like they were parting for a lifetime and not for a night. He knew that feeling well — that we've-been-to-hell-and-back feeling he'd always assumed only cops and military guys got after really close calls. That feeling of having run a gauntlet and barely making it out the other side.

But from the looks of it, civilians could get that feeling, too. Sisters.

He watched Mia glide silently back through the water, a dark splotch in the silvery bay, wondering the whole time how he'd ever been fool enough to let her out of his life. Wondering how the hell he was going to get her back into it, too, because what woman could climb into a kayak and flip her ponytail over her shoulder like she lived this kind of adventure — or misadventure — every day?

The kayak bumped the hull of the little sailboat, and he reached down for the line.

"You been here the whole time?" she asked, climbing up the stern ladder.

"Nah," he lied.

Technically, he could argue that he'd spent most of the time pacing, or at least as much as a man could pace across thirty feet of deck. He didn't like her being out alone in the dark, even with the moon providing some light. He'd popped into the cabin once, too, just to take it all in: the idea of two sisters living in a tiny floating home, thousands of miles away from everything familiar and safe. He'd thumped a couple of bulkheads, too, assuring himself the boat was sturdy. When you were used to hundreds of feet of solid Navy steel, a little boat like *Serendipity* seemed ridiculously fragile. His palm bounced back, though, telling him the little boat was plenty solid, all right.

The pictures hung around the cabin said the same thing. They were like a timeline that showed where the little boat had been and with whom. The wise old salt in the big picture hung in the salon must be the grandfather, and the couple of smiling guys in the more recent pictures must be the cousins who'd brought the boat down to the Caribbean. There was a capable-looking chick wearing a bikini under a half-zipped foul weather jacket, and though the waves in the background looked bigger than a house, she was grinning like it was the greatest day ever. It was one of those big smiles aimed not so much at the camera lens but at a special someone's heart.

Kind of like the way Mia used to smile at him, once upon a time.

Right now, though, Mia was biting her lip, keeping her head down, and avoiding his gaze.

"You okay?"

"I'm good," she mumbled.

Right. Good. That's why her hands were shaking as she tied off the line.

He took her by both hands, sat her down in the cockpit, and sank down opposite her, wondering where to start.

"You want to talk?" he tried.

"No."

Mia shook her head but didn't budge an inch, which he figured meant this was one of those no-means-yes moments.

Not a good thing, because talking... Well, he had a lot in common with a brick wall when it came to that kind of thing.

He scraped his fingers through his hair. Rubbed his face. Wished he could grab a quick shower, or shave, or even swim — anything to avoid the inevitable Talk.

Mia started to rise. "I better check the mooring line."

He tugged her back down. "Mia—"

"Really, I better—"

"We have to talk, Mia."

She stared silently at her feet. He stared, too, because *We have to talk* was about as much as he could summon up. He looked around, wishing for a Cyrano who might whisper the right lines in his ear.

No Cyrano. No buddy, which figured, because it was his buddies who'd gotten him into this mess to begin with.

Which made as good a starting point as any, he supposed.

"That morning in New York..." The morning that started so well and ended so badly. He'd kissed her goodbye, ending their fourth perfect weekend together, and headed off to face yet another Monday, yet another week in what had become a crushing grind. "I wasn't expecting you to be the instructor at that refresher course."

She laughed, low and bitter. "Believe me, I wasn't expecting it either."

He hung his head a little. Obviously, his bright idea not to bring work into their precious time together had been a mistake, because she had no idea he was a cop in the dive squad and he had no idea she was an instructor until they found out the hard way.

He'd hauled his ass into work, replaying her soft touch and her *Hurry home to me, sailor* look all the way. They'd squeezed in another half hour of lovemaking that morning and only forced themselves apart after the snooze alarm went for the fourth time, because who needed breakfast when you could start the day like *that*?

But work was work, and a guy did what he had to do. Which meant meeting his unit and heading over to a pool for one of those useless refresher courses deemed necessary in the wake of the accident a month before.

"Like a refresher course would have saved Lou and Dennis when the shit hit the fan," Ken had said as he stripped down in the locker room and pulled out his trunks.

Everyone had murmured in agreement, except maybe Ryan, because he was leaning back against a locker, eyes shut, only half there because he was still basking in the glow Mia always left him with.

"At least the instructor is cute," Ken sighed. "Did you see her?"

"I think Hayes is dreaming about her right now," Murphy joked.

He cracked one eye open. "Hmm?"

They all laughed. Even if it was aimed at him, he didn't care. He was too blissed out, for one thing, and happy to hear the guys laughing, for another. It had been a pissy month for the squad. A month of grim looks, tight lips, and regrets as every one of them wondered how to turn back the clock and do something differently to save their colleagues' lives.

"Hayes looks like he had a hell of a weekend," Murphy laughed. "Who is she, man? Is it that sweet thing who keeps beating your ass in the pool?"

He shook his head but couldn't wipe the huge grin off his face. It had been a hell of a weekend, and not just for the time they'd spent in bed. They'd wandered around Central Park for half of Saturday, which had been one of those sunny, late winter days that felt like spring could be found right around the corner if only you walked enough. Mia had petted every dog, pointed out shapes in the clouds, and told him about summers spent sailing in Maine on some little boat her grandfather owned. A boat Ryan had never, ever imagined he'd see, not in a million years, because he was so busy marveling at the novelty of a woman who was just as much fun to spend time with outside the bedroom as between the sheets.

She'd dragged him to a museum on Sunday, too. An exhibit of some artist who painted blue horses and yellow dogs and red cows and other kooky shit any ten-year-old could have drawn, except Mia said they were great. She told him all about them, most of which went in one ear and out the other, except for the important stuff. Like how warm her hand was in his as she dragged him from one painting to another. How wide her grin stretched, how bright her eyes shone as she stood speechless in front of each painting before sighing in satisfaction and loping off to the next like a filly who couldn't decide which corner of the pasture had the greenest grass.

He'd still been reliving all that, so it didn't seem that important to stop the guys from joking around, even when they took things a little too far.

"Look at him!" Murphy cackled. "Hayes didn't just get laid, he got done."

"Done good, I'd say," Ken added in his muddy Long Island accent. "Earth to Ryan, hello?"

He waved them off and pulled on his trunks.

"She a talker, Hayes?" Ken pitched his voice high. "Oh, Ryan, baby! Harder, harder!"

It wasn't that far off, actually, but he kept his lips sealed.

"Check his back for claw marks, guys."

He threw his stuff in a locker, knowing they wouldn't spot a thing, because Mia had kept her arms high over her head, clutching the bed posts, trusting every inch of her hot flesh to him. Trusting him to bring them both so high, they could have peeked down at the penthouses of New York.

"No marks. Maybe you weren't man enough to drive her crazy, Hayes."

Oh, he'd driven her crazy, all right. Just like she'd done to him.

The guys kept up the banter all the way through the showers.

"I say," Ken cackled in that crazy laugh of his that hadn't been heard in a dark and dreary month. "It's a good thing Hayes finally got fucked to the eyeballs."

Yes, it was crude. Yes, it was stupid. Yes, he ought to have reined it in before they turned the corner to the poolside and practically bowled over someone walking past. Ryan had to grab the woman's arm to keep her from falling over.

"Sorry!" he blurted, settling her back on her feet.

"No prob—" the woman started to say, flipping the hair out of her face. She stared at him with huge blue eyes. "Ryan?"

"Mia?"

Ken chose just that moment to follow him out of the showers, talking nonstop over his shoulder to the other guys. "Like I said, it's a good thing Hayes finally got fucked to the eyeballs by some pretty little thing. Maybe he'll share some around with you piss-poor..."

Ken trailed off, but Murphy was coming up behind him, grinning a mile wide. "What'd you say her name was, Hayes?"

"Mia!" the dive instructor called from across the pool. "Why don't you bring the squad over so we can get started..."

His gut sank faster than a torpedoed ship as his red-cheeked, outdoorsy, fun-loving girl went white as chalk. Mia clenched her fists and looked at him in a way she'd never done before. Not that *Ryan, I really like you* look.

Not that *Ryan, you're really sweet* look.

More like a *Ryan, you're the scum of the earth* look.

Two more guys piled out behind him, oblivious to what was going on.

"Did you try it with her in the shower, Hayes?"

"Yeah, did you lather her up? Or did she lather you down?"

Someone elbowed the guy into shutting up, but it was too late. Mia's face went from so pale she was practically translucent to raging red, and she stretched tall and bristling and thoroughly outraged.

"So, which of you New York cops do I report sexual harassment to? You?" She stabbed a finger in Ken's direction, then moved on. "You?"

Murphy took a step back and stuck his hands up.

"Or you?" Her eyes narrowed on him. Ryan Hayes, stupidest dumb-ass cop ever to hit the five boroughs, because he'd let one offhand comment snowball into *this*.

Her finger shook slightly, but she stood her ground, because Mia was Mia, and once she started something, she never, ever quit.

He looked at her now, staring at her toes in the moonlight, and waited for her hands to curl into fists and let him have exactly what he deserved.

She didn't and she hadn't, though. She'd turned on her heel, strode to the corner of the pool set up for the course with a whiteboard, and glared. Glared and glared and glared as the other instructor got them into the pool for the first exercise of eight interminable hours of hell, which Mia spent in stone-faced silence, looking at the guys like they were a bunch of miscreants who didn't deserve the time of day. Which they pretty much were.

Even when they came back from a brief lunch break she didn't say a word. And if she noticed the black eye he'd given Ken the second he had the chance, she didn't comment.

Ken had been easy to make up with, even if it took Murphy steering him over after a fifteen-minute cool-down time to force them to try again.

"I'm sorry, man," Ken said. "I didn't think she was your... your... Well, I just didn't think."

Which pretty much summed it up, didn't it?

"Are we good, man?" Ken held out a hand for a fist bump which Ryan halfheartedly returned. Yeah, he and Ken were good. He and Mia, on the other hand...

She sat across from him now, the midnight breeze teasing her hair, casting uncertain shadows over her face. Mia, sitting eighteen inches and a world away from him right now. If only a fist bump were all it took to make them all better again.

"I'm so sorry, Mia."

There it was again, that ridiculously inadequate word.

He'd hung around the pool for an hour after the class ended, waiting for a chance to talk to her, only to be told by the other instructor that she'd left by through the back door.

Classy Mia Whitman, reduced to slinking out the back door. Because of him. The nauseous feeling he'd been fighting all day grew.

Every honk of city traffic, every voice on the street was an accusation as he made his way home at the end of that miserable day. The couple of days he'd given Mia to cool down turned into a week and then into two, and two weeks was too late, because she was gone. The woman who opened the door to the apartment Mia had been subletting only knew that the previous occupant was gone. Where Mia had gone, how he could get in touch, the woman had no clue.

Gone. Mia was just gone. Gone from the pool where they'd done their morning laps. Gone from the apartment. Gone from his life.

The spring that seemed so promising withered away, and winter came back with a vengeance, slushy and cold and gray, especially on weekends when he wondered why the end of a short-term relationship would prompt a thousand mournful questions every day.

"Okay, she was pissed off," Ken had said at around that time. "But didn't she kind of overreact?"

That's what he thought, too. At least at first. But then one utterly depressing Sunday morning that ought to have been a really great Sunday morning he could have spent with Mia if he hadn't been such a dick, he let his itchy fingers do a little snooping on the Internet and followed the hunch that had been growing in the back of his mind.

Mia Whitman, sexual harassment. He typed it in as a search term. Hit enter. Waited.

Nothing.

He stared at the screen for a while then typed again.

Mia Whitman, Olympic swimming. Because a woman who swam like Mia had to have been that good, or at least close, right?

And bingo: pages and pages of swim meet results dating not too far back with Mia's name at or near the top. Lots of top-ten, even top-five results in major collegiate meets with times that made him whistle, they were so fast. He scrolled through another three pages of results before a headline jumped out at him.

Collegiate Swimmer Puts Past Behind Her for a Shot at Olympic Gold.

By the time he got three sentences into that article, his blood was boiling.

For most competitors, this week's Olympic Trials are a chance to realize a dream. For one, it is a chance to escape a nightmare, the article started. *For years, Mia Whitman chased her dreams with an intense training regimen: morning workouts, evening drills, with barely enough time for a shower, meals, and classes in between...*

He skimmed through the next part then slowed down again.

Henry J, a fellow student at Tufts, wired the camera after hours in the showers...

The women's squad couldn't have suspected...

If it had been a newspaper in his hand, he would have crumpled it up and thrown it away, wishing he could take back what the guys in his squad had said.

"Did you try it with her in the shower, Hayes?"

"Yeah, did you lather her up?"

He took five long breaths and read on.

The videos circulated through several fraternities before being brought to the attention of campus police...

Sexual harassment lawsuit filed by head of women's squad...

He shook his head more with every line. It was one of those no-win cases where a woman had more to lose by bringing a man to justice than in letting him get away. But Mia had stuck to her principles, pressing charges and making the case public, thus bringing a maelstrom of exposure upon herself. He could picture the whispered comments she must have had to endure.

"Hey, isn't that the chick from the videos?" some fraternity bastard would snicker on the way to class.

"Hey, baby, want to lather up for me?" the jerk's buddy would add.

Ryan weighed an imaginary bat in his hands and pictured how good it would feel to put it to work on guys like that.

Now she wants to put that all behind her, the article said. *"All I want to do is swim my best," Whitman said, refusing further comment...*

He scrolled ahead, looking for the results of the Olympic Trials. He ran a finger down line after line of names, times, places until he finally found it: Mia Whitman, women's 800m, fifth place. A tight finish in which she'd missed her chance by a fraction of a second. The end of an Olympic dream.

He'd sat in front of the screen for a long time, scrubbing his face so hard, he probably wouldn't have to shave for another couple of weeks.

No, Mia hadn't been overreacting. Not one bit.

Chapter Fifteen

Mia sat very, very still, trying to hold the tears back. A mish-mosh of tears, because no matter how often she told herself the memory of stupid comments wouldn't hurt her, they still did. But at the same time, the sight of Ryan looking at her, droopy and inconsolable as a saggy-eyed basset hound, pulled from a whole different well of sorrow.

She knotted her fingers together and groped for something to say.

"You told them," she said, and it came out somewhere in between a disbelieving whisper and an angry hiss. "You told all those guys at the pool you were sleeping with me!"

Ryan shook his head. "I didn't tell anyone."

God, did he have to look so...tragic?

"They all knew!"

"Not because I said anything, Mia. I swear."

She folded her arms and tried to look convinced of herself. "Sure."

"Mia, when a guy has the best weekend of his life, the men who know him can tell."

Part of her threatened to soften, because it had been the best weekend of her life, too. Their fourth one together, and it just kept getting better each time. Enough that she'd been working up the nerve to tell Ryan about her grand plan. How she'd wrap up the job in New York in another couple of weeks and head to the Caribbean to sail her grandfather's boat. How she really wouldn't mind if he'd visit her on the boat, because maybe they could keep this magical something up for a while longer. Maybe even a lot longer. They could spend some time sailing the Tropics and afterward come back to New York and...

She slammed on her mental brakes. Maybe she'd been dreaming too much. Maybe Ryan wasn't the sweetest guy ever, but just another prick.

"What kind of people do you work with? Hang out with?"

His eyes narrowed and went fierce. "Good people, Mia. Guys who put their lives on the line."

"Yeah, and other peoples' reputations."

His lips quivered but didn't produce a sound, so she went on.

"What they said about me was disgusting. Demeaning. Do you know what it feels like, being the conquest guys congratulate each other on?"

"You are not a conquest, Mia." His voice was low and firm. If she hadn't been so mad, he might even have sounded scary.

"No, I'm just a great weekend fuck."

"I didn't say that!"

"You did! You said—"

"What did I say?" His voice went from harsh to pleading. "Think back, Mia. What did I say?"

"You said... you said..." She clenched her fists and scoured her memory. Hadn't he said... Or maybe he was the one who...

She searched and searched and came up blank.

Okay, maybe he hadn't actually said much.

"Fine. Maybe you didn't say anything, but that's just as bad."

"I didn't know you were right there."

"Exactly my point!" She had to strain not to scream. "Behind my back, you treat me like shit. To my face, you're all kind and nice."

And sweet, her subconscious threw out. *And cute. And really, really sincere.*

"It was a mistake, Mia. A really bad one. I spent the rest of the day shutting them up."

"Very effective," she shot back, although her resolve was wavering.

Ryan's jaw jutted forward. "Ken's black eye. He didn't start the day with that, did he?"

She blinked. There had been a guy with a black eye...

"And Murphy falling in the pool?"

She shrugged. "Very mature."

"Mia, I'm sorry."

"Go back in time and undo it," she said, knowing she had him now.

He wilted. "I can't. But I did make them—"

She cut him off, because she'd heard enough. "Look, Ryan, what are you doing here?"

Other than saving my life, her subconscious pointed out. *Twice.*

God, it was hard to stay mad at him when he was a foot away. She closed her eyes.

Bed. Dropping into bed and turning off her brain had a lot of appeal right now.

"Mia, what the guys said was wrong. That I didn't stop them was wrong." His voice was pinched, like the words had to be forced out. "But we're not complete assholes. Just listen for one second, please."

She kept her eyes closed and her lips squeezed tight.

"I let them get carried away because it was the first time in a month that the guys were laughing again. Loosening up. We'd had a really bad couple of weeks. The accident. The interviews. Recovering the bodies..." His voice cracked just a tiny bit.

Bodies?

"The funerals, the investigations..."

Then it clicked. She'd arrived in New York the week after a terrible accident that killed two members of the dive squad.

Ryan's squad.

Somehow, she'd never made the connection before. She'd mourned the tragedy along with all of New York, but she hadn't known Ryan was a police diver at that point. And when she did find out what he did for work, she'd been too mad to give much thought to the nitty-gritty of his job.

Like wondering what it might be like to recover a body. And not just an anonymous body, but the body of a colleague. A friend. And then she got to wondering a little more, like what if that hadn't been Ryan's first time doing such a gut-wrenching thing. The Navy didn't work in kiddie pools, after all.

Maybe the furious laps he'd swum weren't only about exercise. Maybe the times he'd gone silently distant meant a different kind of time-out.

"None of us wanted to do that refresher training that day. Everyone was in a really crap mood, so when they started joking..."

She watched him scratch at the hem of his shorts while a tiny twitch started up in the outside corner of his left eye. Now he was the one staring at the floor, and she was the one studying him.

Maybe... maybe a guy could be forgiven for not sharing certain things. For letting crude jokes cover the pain of some really bad things.

"I didn't know about the shower video thing, Mia. If I had, I would never—"

Her head jolted up. "You know about that?"

He nodded, looking a decade older. "I'm sorry. Really, really sorry."

Her ribs ached as a familiar flash of anger rose up inside. She wanted to point her finger right in his face and yell, rage, and scream.

But she didn't have it in her. She'd been so mad for so long, she was all worn out.

That, and she'd had a really shitty day. Her skin itched, her muscles ached, and her joints creaked even when sitting still. But no matter how tired she was, she knew she'd never get to sleep. Her body was so out of kilter. Her soul, too.

She put a hand on the deck, because *Serendipity* had a way of calming her, like her grandfather always had. The day she'd run home from college when the whole video scandal broke, her grandfather had come over, hugged her, and led to her dad's liquor cabinet.

We'll deal with this like true sailors, he'd joked, trying to shore her up. *With a good, stiff drink.*

He'd made her feel so grown up, so strong, that in the end, she didn't take the drink. Not even the Irish coffee her granddad had settled on and spent the next hour nursing quietly while he told her sea stories. She'd sat at his feet and petted the dog and let a little bit of goodness creep back in through the pain.

Maybe that would help now: sailor's remedy. A good, stiff drink.

"You want something to drink?" She lurched to her feet so quickly, she nearly bowled Ryan over.

Ryan sitting down was that much shorter than her, and his deep, sad eyes took her in like a faithful old hound. "What do you have?"

She took mental stock. They had a couple of beers, wine in a box, and a little rum, plus the whiskey her cousins Seth and Tobin had left onboard for special occasions. Somehow, she doubted this was the kind of occasion they had in mind, but hell, a shot of whiskey in coffee might just do her good. It certainly couldn't make things worse.

"Irish coffee," she whispered.

"Works for me," he said, so softly she could barely hear.

She went into the tiny galley below, lit the propane stove after priming it exactly the way her granddad always did, and stood staring at the kettle as the water heated up. Then she let her eyes slide closed and her mind go blank, because blank was better than totally messed up.

The water started ticking toward a boil when the companionway stairs creaked. The air behind her warmed, and two tentative arms slipped around her waist so smoothly, she could have sighed. All she had to do was lean back a little and heaven would be hers: her back to Ryan's football field of a chest.

The question was, did she want heaven? Did she trust heaven? Did she trust herself?

She pulled in a deep breath. Let it out again, struggling inside.

She drew another breath, and then she sighed, because it seemed her body had already decided to settle back against him. And damn, that felt good. He rested his chin on her shoulder, his cheek against her ear, and the two of them stood there, breathing as one. On the inhale, his chest rose, and her back followed. On the exhale, a tiny flutter of air warmed her cheek. Inhale: her ribs tightened against his arms. Exhale: his body curled around hers.

The waves rolling over the pebbly beach not too far away did the same. The bay was calm, and *Serendipity* seemed to be nodding off to sleep.

Maybe she didn't have to figure everything out tonight. Maybe all she had to do was breathe and let her mind go blank.

Which was a great plan...theoretically. But blank wasn't coming, not with Ryan standing that close, smelling that sweet.

Chapter Sixteen

Mia breathed him in the way she breathed in starlight on perfect tropical nights: with a long, slow intake that triggered all of her senses, not just the sense of smell. Like the feel of his body heat, seeping over to her. The touch of his thumbs, gently stroking over hers. The sense of the boundaries between their bodies blurring until two were more like one.

The stubble of his cheek scrubbed across her collarbone, lighting a spark that jumped from one nerve to another until her entire body was alive with a sudden, aching need. A need that shoved the pain and anger of the past into a distant corner and pulled the present front and center.

And just like that, nothing else mattered but his touch.

"Tell me to stop," he whispered midnuzzle.

"I don't want you to stop," she breathed.

Ever, an inner voice added. *Never stop and never leave me, even if I'm dumb enough to try to make you go.*

His arms tightened as if in answer. *I will never let you go.*

She tilted her head to drag a little more scrape out of his gentle caress, because that pulled her body back from exhaustion into something closer to bliss.

His lips closed over her ear, tugging the lobe so gently her frown turned into a grin. She tipped her head back, coaxing him closer to her neck, and sighed when his dry lips fluttered kisses along her soft skin.

"Hmm," he mumbled. "You taste good."

She was about to say, *I taste salty*, when he went on.

"You always taste good."

The bass of his voice made her toes curl, and whatever molecules in her body weren't yet on fire ignited and crackled happily alongside with the rest.

Yeah, she could burn up for this man. She could throw her pride to the wind. Could lose herself in this moment and not even feel guilty about it, at least not tonight.

She wiggled her backside against him. "Still got some energy somewhere?"

He answered in a hum. "You give me energy."

She nodded. If they could somehow harness the heat coming off their bodies now, *Serendipity* wouldn't need solar panels.

Her back pressed into him in all the right places, and every atom in her body jumped up and down like the water in the kettle, just beginning to boil.

"Might just put that coffee on hold," she whispered, turning off the burner.

He murmured in agreement and let his hands slide an inch lower, then slide back up. Like a cat, she arched against him, and he hesitated, deciding where to go. Her body was at war with itself, too, making impossible demands like begging his hands to cup her breasts while screaming for them to roam farther south at the same time.

With Ryan, though, nothing was impossible. His left hand slid up and under her bra while his right plunged down, and she moaned in response. A tiny animal moan to tell him he was getting it just right.

"Mia," he murmured, cupping the soft flesh of her breast.

A series of breathless kisses tickled her neck, and she raised her arms, folding them to his shoulders to get them out of the way. She rested her left leg on the step of the ladder, opening her core to him. He ran his left thumb over her nipple at exactly the same moment that the fingers of his right hand slid under the edge of her shorts and teased her folds.

"Ryan," she moaned.

Coffee was definitely, definitely on hold. Maybe forever, if he managed to keep up that heavenly pressure over her clit.

As he pressed down and circled her sex with his whole hand, the fabric of her shorts moved too, sending her higher and higher up the charts. The hard jut of his cock against the small of her back had her rubbing up and down his body. He worked her shirt up to roll and pinch her nipples, and if he kept that up, she'd come screaming like a kettle in no time.

She wanted that. Wanted to come long and hot and hard, but she wanted to come with him. And Ryan, damn him, liked to stretch things out to marathon lengths, which she was just not up for tonight. He'd gotten her flying good and quick; it was time to do that to him, too.

She turned in his arms and dove into a sloppy, soul-licking kiss that made his eyes go wide. She knew; she peeked. When his cock jerked against her stomach, she reached for it. Granted, with a lot less finesse than his own gentle, calculated touches of her body had shown, but Ryan didn't seem to mind. He only protested when she let go.

"Wait," she mumbled, starting again.

This time she slid her hand into his shorts and took him one finger at a time in a wide, loose grip. She didn't have much choice but wide and loose because he was that big and thick. He put a hand over hers and helped her slide up and down at exactly the pace he liked. She went from the broad, throbbing hardness of his cock to the soft skin of his sac and back again, picturing the pleasure every hard inch of him would provide when he drove into her.

Soon. Very soon, she wanted that to happen. Needed it to happen. Her day had been all about survival, and instinct was screaming to take the reins from her mind.

With her free hand, she shoved his shorts lower. She kissed him at the same time and flattened her breasts against the wide expanse of his pecs. She ran her fingers over the tiny grooves in shoulder muscles piled in thick layers that rippled and heated under her touch.

"Need to get rid of this," she grunted, pulling his shirt up.

"And this," he added, working hers up the minute his arms were free.

She folded around him the second she could, caught in a whirling, dizzying tornado she never wanted to escape. Pulling his face to hers with both hands, she pressed into another hungry kiss and consumed him. His skin was salty from their unplanned swim, just like hers, and rubbing against him ignited her like a struck match. She shimmied down, then scrubbed back up, making her nipples peak. She could practically smell the sulfur, see tiny threads of smoke rise from every long, hard scrape. If it hadn't been for the steady sea breeze wafting in from the open cabin door, they might just have burst into flames.

Something fluttered like a flag of surrender. Her bra, discarded to one side.

She peeked up and found Ryan's eyes burning into her like never before.

Mine, they said. *Mine.*

Mine, her body sang back as she explored the delicious curves of his rear. *Mine.*

She'd heard a thousand hushed warnings when she set off for the Caribbean. To watch the wind, the waves, the tide. To be wary of reefs and robbers and sudden storms, and she'd scoffed them all away. But here they were, all those dangers, wrapped in one man. Ryan was the reef that caught her hull and held it fast; Ryan was the thief, and he was sweeping her away. Around the two of them were the wind, the waves, the tide — unstoppable forces of nature propelling them to hidden shores.

But that was only the half of it. The other half was the thrill of surrendering to nature, because nature knew things no mind could grasp. Nature knew about man and woman and the comfort to be found in joining as one. Nature knew that a mind too tired to think could only be soothed by one thing.

Serendipity nodded over the rippling water of the bay, which combined with another movement: Ryan, turning her so her back was to the chart table. He caged her in with his arms, leaning into her space. His wide hands gripped her ribs as his lips worked hers.

"Closer," she insisted, leaning against the solid wood and wrapping one leg around his waist. She still had her shorts on, but that didn't stop her from grinding against his cock. "Closer, Ryan." Her hands slid down his rear and pulled him in.

"Mia." His voice was husky.

Her shorts and panties were the only things keeping them apart, but an onlooker might have overlooked that, the way his hips started thumping against hers.

"God, Mia. You kill me," he murmured. His eyes were at half-mast, his jaw clenched.

"Kill you?"

"In the best possible way," he added, nuzzling her with his grizzly chin.

He hitched her up enough for her left foot to leave the ground, and she snaked that leg up beside the other, making him groan her name again. "Mia."

No one said her name that way. Achy and needy and greedy, too.

He kissed her neck and scraped his teeth against the bare skin, and she tipped her head back for more.

"Lean back," he whispered.

"Back?"

"I got you."

He slid his hands to her back and leaned in, pressing her toward the table.

"Trust me," he whispered.

Trust him? An hour ago, she would have scoffed. Now, she closed her eyes and let him guide her back. Back and back until she thought she'd missed the table, but then it was there, thick and solid behind her shoulders.

"Did I ever tell you how beautiful you are?" he murmured, dropping his head to her breast.

She didn't get an answer out other than a husky moan. He consumed her, sucking in her nipple, letting it pop out, and tugging it with his lips while his hands scooped and molded the yielding flesh and his chin scraped her skin in deliciously rough strokes.

Did I ever tell you how beautiful you make me feel? She tried, but the only sounds she managed were a series of moans and sighs. Topless on the chart table shouldn't feel this good. Too bad she hadn't shed her shorts before she got there.

He thrust against her, and her whole body slid across the chart beneath her. She traveled across it, covering hundreds of miles of open water with one quick slide.

Ryan pulled her hips closer, then pushed forward again, and there she went, skidding from the curve of Central America over to the Antilles. Colombia was under her rear, Jamaica under her right shoulder, and maybe if she let him screw her, hard and hot and searing the way her body begged for him to do, she'd end up with a Caribbean tattoo etched into her skin, complete with islands, lighthouses, and reefs.

She giggled at the image and let her fingers tangle in his hair.

His head popped up. "What?"

"This," she answered, grinning at him.

His eyes flicked over her chest and down her belly. "What?"

"You screwing me on my grandfather's chart table."

His eyebrow jumped up, then curved into a wicked look. "Me about to screw you on your grandfather's chart table, except for two things." He pulled back a little and ran both hands up and down her belly, wrapping his fingers around her ribcage.

"Except what?"

He kissed her belly button, and she thrust her hips up.

"Except you still have your shorts on."

"Easy to fix, officer."

He grinned, and her heart soared. God, a smile looked good on him, erasing the serious for a change.

"That, and the table's a little too high."

"Maybe you're a little too low."

He silenced her with another thrust that rocked her bones.

"I'm not saying it won't work," he said, taking on a cocky little drawl and thrusting again. "What I'm saying is..." He punctuated each phrase with a push of his hips that had her so close to orgasm, she could scream. "But..." He leaned over her and spoke right into her ear, "it won't be just how you like it."

"It won't?" she squeaked. Because what he was doing right now was definitely working for her.

"Not hard enough," he grunted, pushing her into the Atlantic again. His hands grasped her knees and hitched them higher around his waist. "Not deep enough." His cock hammered at her entrance, but he was right. The angle was a little off, their alignment not quite right. "Not the way you need it right now."

"And you know just what I need?" she managed, trying to keep some semblance of control.

He growled his answer. "I do, because I need the same thing."

She tried cocking an eyebrow, but it was hard to do *vixen* from flat on her back.

He straightened, pulled her upright, and tilted his head toward the forward cabin.

"Follow me," he whispered, and the words sparked up and down her spine. "Follow me."

Chapter Seventeen

As it turned out, Ryan followed Mia, but that suited him just fine. Because the sight of her, beckoning him along the narrow hallway of the boat toward the front cabin, worked on more than just his cock. It worked on his soul.

She wanted him. Needed him in a way that went beyond ascents from crazy depths and death-defying escapes and what they were about to do in that bunk tonight. She forgave him, even if he had a lot of apologizing left to do. Which he had a plan for, but that would come later, when the time was right.

This part, this touching and feeling, he hadn't been planning for. Hoping for, sure, but not planning, because he was flying by the seat of his pants, and miracle of miracles, not screwing up for a change. Maybe the moon was playing Cyrano, because he'd actually said a couple of things that came out right. Maybe there was poetry in the plain truth. She really was beautiful, and he really did need Mia more than his next breath of air.

"Right this way, officer," she cooed, waving him along.

He grinned. Maybe he should have told her about his job earlier. This was kind of fun.

"Yes, ma'am," he rumbled, and that wasn't a calculated effect at all. That was Mia, turning him upside down. Again.

She was something, his mermaid-sailor-diving queen. So trim and toned, it would be easy to picture her body tapering into a tail. Her bare breasts were pert and tight, the nipples sweeping up at an angle that begged for his lips. He was already a goner, like he'd been from the very start.

She stopped in the open doorway by the cabin and slid her hands down her sides, finally stripping out of those running shorts. Nice shorts, especially on Mia, but he'd seen enough of them that day. He'd seen enough of all the layers covering her up, in fact. His eyes followed as she slid the shorts down, inch by luscious inch, flipping every switch in him to full steam ahead.

He stepped forward, closing the distance, and Mia stepped back into the cabin, opening the gap up again. One step forward for him, another step back for her. Forward. Back. He had to stoop because the ceiling was lower in the bow. She retreated right against the high captain's bunk that took up the entire cabin and scooted onto it, butt first, legs following, knees apart. His cock twitched, taking in that view.

"You kill me," he muttered, shaking his head.

"In the best possible way, right?"

Even in the darkness of the cabin, he could see her eyes sparkle. The moonlight shone in through an overhead hatch, lighting different parts of her as she slid back. When her face retreated into the dimmer part of the cabin, the moonlight danced over her nipples. When she edged back, it shone on the checkerboard of her taut middle in a bold show of sheer feminine power. She was muscled inside, too, and the thought of her tight sheath clenching down over his cock…

He'd been holding back, stretching the anticipation out, but something in him cracked, and suddenly he was prowling into that den of a cabin after her, climbing over her body in one quick move. He crushed his mouth to hers, swallowing her up. His chest squeezed against the soft pillow of her chest, his legs found their way between hers, and his cock honed in on home.

"No condom," he muttered, hoping to hell it didn't matter. She was on the pill, and they had both checked out clean, so they'd taken to going without condoms in New York.

"No problem," she breathed, wrapping her arms and legs around him. Her fingers roamed, setting off sparks like a test sequence of every one of his nerves. "Ryan…"

One little push, and he'd be in heaven, because she was wide open and slick and ready for him. A roaming finger told him as much, but he held back, using his last strand of self-restraint.

"Ryan," she moaned, shoving her hips up. "Don't play with me."

"I'm not playing," he grunted. "I want to be in you. Need to be in you, but I need this, too."

This was the sight of her, stretched willingly beneath him, ready to come undone. *This* was her eyes and her voice and her body, straining for him. *This* was the assurance that it wasn't just about tonight.

A thousand words backed up in his throat, but none of them had worked up the nerve to venture out first.

"Mia. . ."

She slipped her arms off his back and cupped his face with both hands, pulling him down slowly until they were nose-to-nose.

"I get it, Ryan," she whispered. "I get it."

He got stuck on his next breath because his heart and lungs were so busy tap-dancing that everything else went by the wayside for a second. Maybe the two of them didn't need fist bumps or dolphin squeaks. Maybe they just needed to shut up and let that natural harmony that sprang out of nowhere do the talking, the way it always did when they got close.

A good thing Mia kissed him then, because it helped loosen the choked-up feeling in his throat. When she let him go, she wriggled her hands overhead, a signal for him to pin them down, and arched her back, raising her body against his.

He gave himself a mental shake. Right. Sex. He supposed to be fucking her, not admiring and loving and marveling at the crazy ideas she sent careening through his mind. Like having lots of Sunday mornings together and lots of weekend walks. A lifetime of them.

"Ryan," she breathed.

He let himself admire for one more second. Then, with one smooth slide, he was in. In her; in heaven. Same thing.

"Yes!" Her voice wavered as he plunged in.

He slid good and deep and stayed rooted for a long minute, breathing her in. Then he withdrew all the way to her entrance, where the tip of his cock burned and begged and pleaded before he gave in and dipped back in.

"Ryan..." Her fingers tightened around his.

He found a rhythm, sliding in and out, faster and faster until even Mia was breathing in little pants and grunts that were a lot more caveman than elite swimmer. She hitched her feet higher until they were planted on the low ceiling so she could meet his strokes with little thrusts of her own.

"That's so good," she breathed, twisting her head from side to side. "So good."

He was pretty sure that line had featured in his dreams during those lonely weeks they'd spent apart. He made that his quest: to see Mia writhing and moaning and totally undone, all because of him. And if it meant he'd also be writhing and moaning and coming totally undone, well, that was just fine, because this was one of those win-win deals where everyone came out ahead.

When she clenched her inner muscles around him, he just about howled. Just about let it all go right there, but he managed to channel it into an urgent series of sharp thrusts that built on each other until he was hammering both of them right up to the blurry edge of pleasure and pain.

Mia threw her head to the side and cried out his name, God's name, and a whole lot of other gratifying sounds. He rode an out of control wave that built and built until there was no holding back. His balls pinched just as Mia contracted under him.

"Yes!" she cried, clutching his shoulders, squeezing inside.

He was going, going, gone, possibly making a few caveman noises himself. He shook, he spilled, he sighed, and then sank down over her, totally spent.

He huffed and puffed into her neck for an eternity, stroking her collarbone, murmuring something unintelligible in her ear, or her chest, or whatever part that was pillowing his head. It didn't seem to matter, what with him floating next to her in a glowing neon bubble of bliss. His limbs were warm and leaden and tired in a satisfyingly boneless way. His arms felt thick, his thoughts muddled. Time slowed down along with his breath until even that didn't matter any more. There was just her, warm and soft and snuggly, and him.

A light zephyr spun the boat in a lazy circle, and it turned gracefully on its tether. Nodding. Humming, almost. Whispering him to sleep.

Chapter Eighteen

There was a certain kind of magic to sleeping on a boat. A feeling of disconnecting from the rush and fuss and mess of humanity. Of seeking comfort in the lap of the earth. The water, the wind, the fresh air; it made a person feel alive.

And never so alive, despite the sore muscles, than this morning, Mia decided.

She'd slept the best kind of sleep: deep and dreamless. She might have slept forever had it not been for the gentle tap of morning light on her cheek. The sun rose and set every day, but on a boat, it felt like a miracle every time — even more so the morning after she'd nearly been killed twice.

She cracked an eye open, then let it slide shut and slowly, slowly took stock.

Ryan's breath came in warm little puffs against her shoulder, deep and regular with the serenity of sleep. His arm was looped over her side, his hand loose at her belly, giving her space but hanging on just tight enough to keep her near.

She curled her fingers through his — slowly, carefully, so as not to wake him up — and squeezed just enough to assure the last of her fluttering nerves that everything was all right. He was all right. There'd been that terrifying moment after they'd been run down in the dinghy when she couldn't tell if he was breathing. So she listened and counted his breaths and sent a little prayer to heaven for every one.

Too many near misses. Too much had gone wrong. It was like a malicious wind had set in, determined to sweep her away. Seeing Ryan, then running out of air, then being run down...

She should have been shaking, but the calm of morning and the calm of the man lying at her side made everything seem all right. A yawn and an irrepressible stretch took over her body, rippling through her from head to toe. Then she sighed and settled back against Ryan, stroking his hand.

Serendipity barely bobbed, and she closed her eyes, tuning in to the boat. She had so much to be grateful to her grandfather for: the fun, the adventures, the unconditional love. That feeling of having a compass when she needed it most. The boat was the least of the things her grandfather had gifted her with, though. He'd given her time to take stock of a crazy couple of months. Time to get to know her sister all over again. And now this. A quiet morning with Ryan, the kind she thought she'd never get again.

She thought it was the gentle rocking of the boat at first, but it seemed Ryan was stroking her hand, too. Just one thumb, strumming hers slowly like the E string on a guitar.

"Hmm," she sighed quietly. "Nice."

Being anchored in a hidden cove off a tropical island shouldn't have reminded her of a quiet Sunday morning in New York. But in some ways, the forward bunk felt just like those perfect weekends in New York. The same sleepy feeling of contentment. The same tingle of anticipation in her bones.

Maybe it wasn't the place. Maybe it was the guy. She could snuggle with him on an Arctic ice floe and it would still feel this good.

She wiggled backward, erasing the last empty spaces between their bodies. His fingers knotted around hers then left them for the taut skin of her belly. Hunger might register there soon, because it had been hours since her last meal, but not yet. Not that kind of hunger, anyway. Because the more he stroked, the more a tiny, licking flame built under that warm point of contact and spread throughout her body, so that even parts he wasn't touching felt good.

A low, growly rumble came through her back. Ryan shifted to get closer, working his coarse thumb over skin that felt like it had survived a long drought to finally taste rain.

"Hmmm," she mumbled, making sure he knew it was good.

She guided his hand higher until he caressed the lower edge of her breast. Her left leg went exploring in the meantime, something she barely registered until it was wound snugly behind his and reporting all kinds of good things to be discovered back there.

"Mia," he whispered, and it was like a poem, all in one word.

She wiggled lower, maneuvering the rest of her breast into the hand doing all kinds of amazing things to her as it grazed back and forth. Wishing she had a little more to offer him there, hoping to hell it was good enough.

His fingers showed no signed of stopping. It was only his voice, slowing things down. "You sure you want this?"

It was just like the first time they'd slept together, when she was the one practically tearing his clothes off with her teeth, and he was the one showing a little restraint.

"I'm sure." God, she was sure. It was about the only thing she was sure of right now.

"What if you decide you hate me later?"

She twisted in his arms and caught his face in both hands. No tease, no innuendo. Just her heart and soul on a platter, for him to take or reject. "I never hated you. I never will. And I promise—"

He put his fingers over her lips before she could say the rest. Like he wasn't quite ready for what she might say to him just then.

So she parked the thought in the back of her mind, saving it for a time that wasn't the heat of the moment, when he'd know she meant every word. *Ryan, I want you. I want us.*

Anyway, he was right. She didn't have to talk to show trust and forgiveness. She opened her mouth and caught his finger with her lips. Licked it, up, down, and around while her right leg looped over his.

The emerald eyes blazed and said, *Mia, be sure.*

She tilted her chin up, leaned in, and showed him just how sure she was by diving in with a deep, hard kiss. She slid her tongue inside, finding the soft, cushiony curves beneath. That was Ryan: hard and uncompromising on the outside, yielding and sweet underneath. The trick was getting past the outer armor, but once she was in... She sighed.

When she pulled back for a breath, his eyes were smoldering, his jaw set hard. He ran a hand over her stomach, working her flat against the mattress as his eyes swept over her chest.

"Like this," he said, rising to kneel over her. Hunched, because the ceiling was that low. His eyes glimmered with some deliciously wicked vision as he bunched the pillows and blankets along her side. His hands smoothed her shoulders, then scooped behind them and lifted her up.

A rush of warmth shot through her veins as she realized what he was planning, knowing just how good it would feel.

"This okay?" he grunted, tucking the pillows under her back, making her arch.

"This is great," she mumbled, letting her head fall back, her legs fall apart. Opening up to him in every way possible as he finished arranging the cushions under her back.

There was a yoga pose like this, she vaguely remembered: body arched back over a pillow, chest open to the sky. Something supposedly good for breathing and relaxing and centering or something like that.

Which was all very nice, but it took a former Navy SEAL to teach her what else the position was good for. The one time they'd done this in New York — one of the rare times she'd been content to settle back passively and let him have his wicked way — it had been so good, she'd left the apartment shamefaced from all the noise she'd made. But this time, they were the sole boat in a quiet anchorage far from the beaten track.

Oh, yes. This was going to be good.

Ryan smoothed his hands over her chest, studiously missing her breasts each time.

"You are not going to tease me again," she groaned.

He rocked back on his heels and looked at her, dead serious. "No," he said. "I'm not."

One more sweep of hands, and then he ducked down and ravaged her like a hungry pirate, plucking at her nipples, nipping her lips. He gathered up the loose flesh of her breasts in greedy handfuls and worked them so hard, her cries filled the cabin.

"Okay?" He looked up, barely waiting for her nod before diving straight back to work.

She thought she couldn't get any higher, but then his hands worked down her belly and his head followed.

She moaned even before his tongue made contact, and then she moaned even more, because that marauding tongue was very, very insistent, and very, very skilled. Being ravished really shouldn't feel this good, but with Ryan, giving herself utterly, totally over felt absolutely right.

Trust. The kind of miracle she'd never really considered, just like the sunrise. But now that she took notice, it seemed like the most beautiful thing. Or the second most beautiful thing, because his tongue explored deeper, pushing coherent thought right out of her mind.

Her orgasm came out of nowhere to blindside her, a freight train of clenched muscles and strangled breath and keening cries that carried her a mile down the tracks before throwing her limp and panting to one side, leaving her wondering where the hell she was.

She opened her eyes, found Ryan holding her, and just like that, she knew just where she was.

Home.

One side of Ryan's mouth curled up but not the other, like he wasn't sure smiling was permitted. On the rare occasions when he really smiled a full, unguarded smile, it felt like the sun beaming back into the universe after an eclipse. Another one of those miracles she'd be sure to appreciate from now on.

"Come to me," she whispered, tugging on his shoulders, and he did.

She'd bet good money that no couple in the history of mankind had orgasms that far apart and still called it bliss, because she was utterly spent. But Ryan was only getting started. She lay back doing nothing but feeling the hard slide of him inside her, listening to his heavy breath, letting her hands dance over his back as he thrust into her again and again.

"Mia," he groaned, going stiff all over.

The muscles in his face tightened, one by one, and veins rose up along the arms bracketing her sides. His warm heat engulfed her as his cock pulsed deep, deep inside. It was as close to a miraculous out-of-body experience as she ever wanted to get, and it was so, so good. So good, she managed to rouse one last shred of energy and meet his final thrust.

He groaned; she howled; then they were both panting into the sheets. The boat slid sideways on the mooring, and a single shaft of sunlight traced the line of Ryan's back. She followed it with her hands, sheltering him from it, then pulled a loose sheet over the both of them, huddled in a limp heap.

Reality was out there. Reality was waiting.

She pulled the sheet higher. Let reality wait, just a little bit.

Chapter Nineteen

"I owe you an Irish coffee," Mia sighed.

"I'm good with this." Ryan reached for the mug she offered, put it on the chart table, and pulled her into his arms. "And this."

He was crushing her just a tiny bit, but he had to, because the day they had ahead of them might be as crazy as the day before, and he wasn't heading into it without this.

When she nodded, her hair tickled his cheek. "This is good."

He held her tighter. Yeah, it was good. Great. So great, they were likely to have to have another long talk when they finally got more pressing problems off their plate. A talk he might not mind too much, if she was thinking what he was thinking. That this wasn't just a crazy interlude, but a new beginning. A second chance.

They sat over a silent breakfast in the cockpit, which was just about as similar to New York as Saturn was to Mars. The air was salty, a gull cried overhead, and the sun was sneaking along the scrub-lined hills, sparkling off the calm water.

"So peaceful," Mia murmured.

He scanned the cliffy sides of the bay. Other than a darting bird among the bushes, there was no movement, no hint of trouble. But trouble was out there somewhere, that was for sure.

"Me and Meredith, we can sit in the cockpit for hours, just looking at it. Not taking pictures, not reading, not doing anything but just looking."

He suspected he could do the very same thing, for days, even weeks, especially if she were there with him. But this was her adventure, and her sailboat, and not his. He'd managed to drag a week off work at short notice to come track her down, but even if she wanted to let him stick around, he couldn't.

Which meant it was his turn to sigh. Guys like him didn't take months off at a time. They worked their jobs, year in, year out, and squirreled away their savings in tiny little bits so that maybe in retirement they might rent a trailer not too far from the water and pretend it was a place like this.

Still, a guy could dream.

"You and your sister..." He changed the subject. "You're kind of alike, but you're so different, too."

Mia chuckled. "Different, for sure."

"She seems a bit more...anxious than you," he ventured.

Mia flashed a bittersweet smile. "If there's a cloud on the horizon, Meredith sees a storm. You get the slightest cut, and she treats it like the first sign of the plague." Her face darkened. "She wasn't always that way, but then..." She trailed off, looking sadly at the horizon, and he had to wonder what the *then* was.

"Anyway," Mia continued, hitting a lighter tone. "You give her a boat to steer or a life-threatening emergency with lots of blood, and she's a rock. Broken bones, bleeding wounds, no problem. Cooking, too. She's a really good cook."

He laughed. "I'd say that's a good start. Plus she can sail like Captain Cook. You, too."

Mia shook her head. "Everything else, though, and her confidence goes down the drain. Like she's a failure before she even tries. She takes care of everybody but herself, as if she doesn't deserve anything more than what she has."

Now he really wanted to know what the *then* in her past was, but Mia sighed, shook her head, and stared into the distance, where the aquamarine shallows turned to deeper blues and grays that melted right into the horizon.

He looked, too, and pushed thoughts of painful pasts away to try to focus on promising futures filled with fantasies like having a boat, a horizon to point it toward, and Mia to share it all with. He closed his eyes on the shimmering waves of heat building over the island and let the fantasies grow. A little time sailing with Mia would be perfect. Then both of them could head back to New York, and when they were ready, they could move to Florida for that dive salvage job with slightly better pay, slightly saner hours, and a lot more private time. Maybe even family time.

Then he forced his eyes back open, because a man could dream himself right onto a reef if he didn't watch out.

He tried joking the choked-up feeling away. "Imagine a guy like Stanley here."

Mia snorted. "Watching the world through his camera lens."

He held up an imaginary camera, happy for the distraction, and trained it on her. "Good morning, Mia!" he said, imitating Stanley's high-pitched voice. "How about you shatter the silence of this beautiful place by telling us all about it?" He panned along the boat. "Tell us everything we can see with our two eyes, please."

He focused the imaginary camera back on her then stopped. *Oh, shit.*

Mia was frozen, her face completely still. She wasn't even meeting his eyes, just staring into nothingness over his shoulder.

God, he was an idiot. He'd stuck an imaginary camera in her face and brought back the ugly memories and ruined everything and—

"Stanley," she croaked.

Stanley?

She waved vaguely behind him. "The camera."

Stanley and his camera? "What?"

Her eyes focused on him, shining bright now with some realization, some hope.

"Stanley was videoing everything! He was filming over your side of the dive boat, where that other boat was moored."

He froze while the gears ticked over in his mind. "The boat with the two guys..."

"The guys that sped off right before the explosion," she finished, looking grim. "If they show up on Stanley's footage..."

"We would have a new suspect for the cops."

Neither of them moved for a second, but then they both jumped up and started hustling around. They rushed through breakfast and the quickest, most water-efficient shower he'd had since leaving the Navy before finally paddling the kayak to shore.

They scaled the hill and looked left. Nothing but deserted road, with an endless brown-green carpet of cactus and scrub thrown over the hills.

They looked right. More of the same.

For getting away from prying eyes, the place was perfect. For getting back to town, however...

"Uh-huh," Mia nodded into the phone in her second call to Meredith of the morning, trying to track Stanley down. "When? This morning? Where?"

From the sounds of it, Stanley wasn't that easy to find.

"What?" Mia yelped.

"What did Meredith say?" he asked when she finally hung up.

"She said a couple of cruise ships came in, and the noise from all those tourists made Stanley and Brenda move to a quieter hotel on the north end of the island."

"That's good, right? It's closer to here."

"Close," Mia murmured. "But maybe not close enough." She trotted out into the middle of the deserted road and looked around, waiting for a miracle ride. "When Meredith asked the hotel in town about Stanley, you know what they said?"

"What?"

She paused, then shook her head. "They said, 'What a popular guy! Two men were just here looking for him.'"

His heart thumped harder in his chest. "They could be any two men."

She nodded. "Could be. But if they're the wrong two men..."

He looked left, then right. "Then we need to make tracks."

Easier said than done, because they were in the middle of nowhere with no transportation. He had no backup, no badge, no jurisdiction.

Mia set off at a trot, and he fell into step beside her. Because that was the other thing: he had no choice.

<h1 style="text-align:center">Chapter Twenty</h1>

"Thank you!" Mia waved as the pickup drove off.

"Thanks!" Ryan echoed. A damn good thing that sheepish-looking couple in a rental had come by when they had, looking like they'd had a memorable night under the stars, or they'd never have made it to the hotel in time.

In time for what, he wasn't quite sure, only that he had the foreboding sense of a loudly ticking clock. They had to get to Stanley's footage before anyone else did.

Mia dusted her shirt off and swiped at his back. "Gotta look like we belong here," she murmured, nodding to the hotel.

It was an upmarket, four-story place perched on a solitary hill with a view of the ocean so big it reminded him how small Bonaire really was. Twenty-four miles long and only a couple wide didn't leave a lot of space — or time — to outwit the bad guys.

"Let's go." He nodded toward the entrance. "Act like you belong here."

Which Mia could easily pull off, because she was the type who could fit in anywhere in the world, from seedy backpacker joints to luxury hotels.

He grabbed her hand. "Make like we're honeymooners, okay?"

Her eyes went wide, and his blood warmed up at the idea. Him and her coming to a place like this, not to save their asses but to celebrate forever.

His fingers tightened around hers, and then he shook his head. *Focus, Hayes. Focus.*

"We're honeymooners about to mix up our room number."

"We're what?"

"Just follow my lead," he said, trying to act like he knew exactly what he was doing. Which was a stretch, because no job he'd ever worked involved sneaking into hotel rooms. "What room did Meredith say?"

"413."

He stuck on what he hoped was a goofy honeymooner grin as they entered the cool lobby and approached the front desk. The key to 413 was dangling on a hook, which meant Stanley and Brenda were out diving or eating or, knowing Stanley, filming Brenda diving or eating. Which suited Ryan just fine, because it was easier this way. They'd go in, grab the video, and then head back to town to give it to the police. Not exactly proper procedure, but with a ticking clock, he had to improvise.

Of course, video would only help if Stanley actually managed to capture a shred of evidence, but he'd cross that bridge when he came to it. And if all those bridges he had been accumulating were lining up one behind the other, well, he'd just have to do his best.

Luckily, there were several couples checking out and only one overwhelmed clerk working the front desk.

"Room 413, please," he said.

And just like that, he had Stanley's key in his hand.

"Easy," he whispered as they walked to the elevator, trying not to run.

"Right," Mia murmured. He could feel the shake in her hand. "Easy."

There was no one in the hallway of the fourth floor, so letting themselves into the room was easy, too. The bed was unmade and a suitcase stood propped open against a wall, overflowing with discarded clothing. The sliding door to the balcony was open, and the curtains danced on a light breeze. Strewn across the desk were half a dozen memory cards beside a laptop. From the looks of it, Stanley had been replaying his footage last night.

Mia picked up an unmarked memory card and examined it. "God, which one is it?"

He stuck one into the computer — thank goodness Stanley was one of those leave-the-laptop-on-at-all-times guys — and clicked on the picture file.

Mia ran a finger along the thumbnails, studying the dates.

"Too early," he said. "Next one."

"Jesus, Stanley takes a lot of footage," Mia grimaced.

"Let's just hope he keeps the camera out of the bedroom." Because Stanley and Brenda in bed together, he really didn't need to see.

"Next," Mia said, handing him another.

They tried the next one and the next and the next.

"Bingo." Most of the files dated from the day before. He clicked on one after another, trying to find the right time.

Footsteps sounded in the hallway outside, and they both jerked their heads up. He held his breath. Mia went stiff as a tree.

The footsteps thumped past the door and carried straight on down the hall.

Whew. The curtain to the balcony flickered, chuckling at how jumpy they were.

He bent back over the screen. *Focus. . .*

"That was the morning dive," Mia murmured, nodding him on.

He skipped through what seemed to be at least an hour of lunch footage and a walk down the town streets, all in double time, and skipped forward some more.

"There!" Mia pointed.

He played the video in regular time, watching the dive group file onto the launch past a grinning Lucky, a jovial Hans, and a breezy Mia. Saw a brief glimpse of himself, hidden in the hoodie, keeping a low profile for as long as he could.

Mia stiffened next to him. God, what had he been thinking, surprising her out of nowhere like that?

". . .the past twenty-six years," Hans said in the video. "Which makes us. . . how much older than you?"

It was weird, watching yesterday play out in front of his eyes. A yesterday that felt a lifetime ago.

The Mia beside him was silent and serious; the Mia on the video was perky and upbeat. "Younger, Hans," she answered Hans. "Your business is younger than me by two years."

"There — look!" Mia — real-time Mia — jabbed a finger at the screen.

He caught a bare hint of movement in the background, and then it was gone.

"Back it up," she urged.

He rewound it a few seconds and kept his finger over the Pause button this time.

"Your business is younger than me—"

He stopped it there, because there was an aluminum dive launch in the background with one man standing at the stern and another in the water. The shot was too blurry to make anything out, so he nudged the footage forward, frame by frame, until he got one that was a little clearer.

"Him," Mia muttered, watching a guy in full dive kit reach up for something the second man handed down.

Then the camera jerked away, and he let the scene play on.

"As for me..." Hans winked in the video. "I was born in Holland a long, long time ago, but I swear I'll die on Bonaire! Just not anytime soon, I hope!"

He watched Mia step sideways through the camera view, saying, "And our last guest today..."

Pausing the video on the moment when he was about to catch Mia totally, unfairly off guard — God, what an idiot — was the last thing he wanted to do, but the camera had the diver in the upper right corner of the frame again, so he had no choice.

The diver strapped a bulky bag to his body and swam away from the launch as the other watched.

"Full wetsuit," Mia murmured, watching the screen. "Diving alone."

He nodded at a pink splotch on the hull. "What's that logo on the boat?"

"I don't know—"

Something scratched at the hotel room door, and both of them froze.

The doorknob jiggled.

After a pregnant pause, it jiggled again. Not the firm turn of the rightful occupant but a secretive try. Mia glanced at him with a wild expression that said, *Oh, shit.*

She scurried to the peephole of the door and immediately spun back to him, making wild chopping motions with her hands.

"Not Stanley and Brenda?" he whispered as she tiptoed back over.

The scratching at the door continued. Someone playing with the lock.

Mia shook her head. "Two guys. Oh, God! Hurry!"

He ejected the card from the laptop, grabbed her hand, and raced for the balcony.

"Now what?" Mia cried, looking out at a dead end, four stories over a very hard fall.

Chapter Twenty-One

There was an audible click as the door lock was sprung. Mia gasped, and Ryan flattened her against the outer wall, out of sight of whoever it was entering the room.

The men who'd tried to kill her — twice — yesterday. She was sure of it. She leaned over the railing and eyed the long drop.

If the hotel had been one of those blocky new constructions where the balconies wrapped all the way around, it would have been easy to scurry away. But this was an elegant place with small, wrought-iron balconies that stuck out like tiny diving boards separated by wide gaps of very thin air.

"Shh!" Ryan hummed in her ear.

Shh was all very well, but they had to get the hell away, because she could hear heavy footsteps clomping across the room and the door to the hallway click shut.

"There!" a low voice growled.

A clicking noise ensued: the shuffle of memory cards on the table.

If the two men were thorough in their search, they'd ransack the room and peek out onto the balcony, too. It was only a question of time. She and Ryan had to get away, and soon. But how?

She leaned farther over the railing and immediately felt sick. Not so much from the height as the utter lack of options. The next balcony seemed miles away, and the one underneath them was filled with deck chairs, a table, and not-quite-empty glasses of champagne. Not even a cat could make a clean, quiet landing there.

Ryan's hard shoulder leaned against hers as he took in the same view.

"That way." She nodded toward the neighboring balcony and threw a leg over the rail.

So easy to decide; so hard to do. Mia eased her body weight over the rail and clung to it for her life. It was a long, long way down to the stone terrace below, where silverware clinked from the last guests eating breakfast.

An angry mutter came from within the room, along with the dull skid of a memory card tossed across the table. Time was running out.

If there'd ever been an unnecessary comment made in the world, it was the one Ryan uttered next.

"Careful!"

Like she would leap from balcony to balcony in any other way.

The railing was nearly flush with the edge of the balcony, giving her about half an inch to perch on before she leaped. Mia eyed the distance. Took a deep breath. Wondered when she'd last told her mother she loved her.

And jumped.

The air seemed awfully thin in the long second she spent clinging to nothing but hope. Then her knee slammed into metal and her hands clawed and her shoulders flew forward and she was hanging on for dear life. Ryan thunked into the railing beside her with a low grunt, and the two of them clung to the side of the safety rail you never want to see, looking at each other.

"Nothing to it," she tried and climbed into the right side of the balcony.

Which hadn't really gained her much more than a wildly accelerating heart rate, because the door to that hotel room was locked. As wide as the gap to Stanley's balcony had seemed when she was jumping, it wasn't enough. Not nearly enough if the two men came out armed and trigger-happy.

"Go! Go!" Ryan hissed, already climbing over the rail to jump to the next balcony.

Mia climbed after him, hoping the second time would be easier. She looked down. Looked across. Touched her bruised knee. Gulped.

No, it wasn't easier. Not one bit.

But she did it anyway, and crashed against the railing in exactly the same way, except for two things. This time, she smashed her right shin. And this time, just as she was ready to exhale, the inch of ledge crumbled under her and she fell.

There was a sickening jolt and a harsh scrape as her legs dropped from under her. Then it was just her and way too much space and limbs that flailed like a cartoon character's. Her shoulders screamed in their sockets when she came to a jarring stop, gripping the wrought iron for her life.

Time slowed as she swung from the lowest part of the rail, suspended by one hand, four stories up.

"Mia!"

She looked up and found Ryan bug-eyed and white, reaching for her free hand. God, his eyes were green. God, his hand was big. God, his legs were long—

He hauled her up and squeezed her to his side.

"Jesus," he whispered.

But whispering was kind of pointless now, because they'd made enough noise to draw a shout from Stanley's room.

Ryan half shoved, half lifted her over the rail. She yanked at the sliding doors. Locked. God, did the hotel guests actually predict someone would come jumping from rail to rail to break into their rooms?

She contemplated smashing the glass, but Ryan pointed to the next balcony one level down.

"Are you nuts?" she hissed.

Voices sounded from Stanley's balcony.

"We need to get off this floor!"

"Hey!" someone barked from Stanley's balcony. Not the voice of the maid or Stanley, that was for sure.

Mia scrambled over yet another railing, ignoring the scrapes and bruises crying from all over her body, and judged the distance.

"Stop!" a man shouted from above.

Very good advice, if it hadn't been coming from the guy who'd cut her air hose one hundred feet underwater and run down her dinghy at night. A guy pulling a gun from his pocket, as a wild glance back revealed.

Ryan launched himself with a grunt, landed in the center of the balcony like a panther, and turned. On one hand, he made it look easy. On the other, it seemed like suicide. She was no panther. She was no Marine or SEAL or whatever the heck he'd been in whatever branch of the military. She was just Mia.

Ryan shoved a chair aside, making space. "Come on!"

"Stop!" the man behind her barked.

Mia was no expert, but she was pretty sure the click she heard was the cock of a loaded gun.

She jumped. Reached. Strained every muscle, focusing on Ryan's outstretched hand. She squinted, too, as if seeing less would help her avoid the spitting *Thwat!* of a silenced bullet, slicing very close to her ear.

She crashed into Ryan, bowling him over like a flying hippo, but that was fine. She'd made it, right?

Ryan scrambled to his feet and pushed her through the — thank you, Lord — open door of the room that some off-task corner of her mind calculated must have been 319. Like they'd be calling room service or something on their way out.

"Oi!" A hefty woman in a pink cleaner's outfit flattened herself against the wall.

"'Scuse me," Ryan murmured, racing past.

"Pardon us," Mia yelped as he towed her along.

Ryan dashed across the hallway, kicked open the fire exit door, and started leaping down whole flights of stairs, which seemed like kid's stuff after the monkey act they'd pulled off outside. When he pushed open the door at the bottom and skidded across the waxed floor of the lobby, a dozen heads turned. He led her onward, hurtling over suitcases, bumping past bellboys, and barely missing vases stuffed with fragrant flowers Mia really would have liked to stop and sniff.

Another time, maybe.

They sprinted for the front doors, then pulled to a screeching stop outside.

No taxi. No friendly couple in a pickup. No saddled ponies ready to help them make a quick escape.

Nothing but a white Hyundai with a pink hibiscus painted on the side, parked far across the way, and a neat row of pastel-colored mopeds, all leaning at exactly the same angle. All except the one an attendant was showing to a guest, a little apart from the next.

"You start it like this," the attendant said as the lobby behind them erupted into shouts. The two men chasing them had burst on to the scene.

Ryan darted for the moped and Mia followed, wishing she had a better plan.

"'Scuse me," Ryan grunted, grabbing for the bike.

"Pardon me," she squeaked, jumping on the seat behind him. If they were going to barge in on maids and steal rental vehicles, at least they could be polite.

"Hey!" the guest shouted.

"Sorry!" She clung to Ryan as he shot down the lane. Her arms circled around his steely torso and hung on tight. "Go! Go!"

The engine of the moped screamed into high gear.

No helmets. No rental contract. No safety briefing. God, they'd have a lot of explaining to do if they survived this day.

The driveway filled with shouts, cries, and the sound of a car engine gunned to life by a hasty hand.

"Faster!" she shouted in Ryan's ear, even though that was about as necessary as him telling her to jump carefully. "Faster!"

Chapter Twenty-Two

Ryan kept one eye on the narrow road, one on the side mirror, and his fingers dug into the grips. Was this as fast as the scooter could go?

"I think that cement truck we passed might have held them up," Mia shouted in his ear.

He still kept the throttle jammed as far as it would go, which could never be fast enough. Too bad the hotel didn't rent 750cc Harleys. He could have borrowed one of those instead of this...this... He groaned, glancing down at the frame.

"What?" Mia peeked over his shoulder.

He pointed at the label. *Kymco Agility 50cc.*

He had to look twice to make sure there wasn't a zero missing. How were they supposed to make their escape with fifty fucking cc's?

The little scooter did its best, though, kicking up pebbles and dust as it hammered along the dirt road. Two bumpy miles later, they came to a paved road and a sign.

Rincon 2km, Kralendijk 17km.

Ryan did a quick calculation. That translated to about twelve miles of hoping this wheezing moped could save their asses.

Great.

Twelve miles was a long way to go, because even a three-cylinder Hyundai could catch them on the open road. And seventeen kilometers was a lot of open road.

About the only thing he liked about this scenario was Stanley's media card in his pocket and Mia's arms around his waist.

She laid her cheek flat against his shoulder, and even if she did it to create a more aerodynamic shape, he liked the idea that she did it just... because. Because she felt as good leaning up against him as he felt having her there.

He glanced in the side mirror, and shit, there was the white Hyundai with the pink flower again. He leaned over the handlebars and willed the moped along.

A long right curve led to a lusher patch of green and the soaring towers of a church, standing prim white against the pale blue sky. Before he knew it, another sign blurred by.

"Rincon!" Mia exclaimed.

He glanced back at her. *So?*

"It's an old town. One of the oldest in the Caribbean, originally settled by the Spanish. Everyone says it's beautiful."

He looked ahead. Beauty, he already had on the back of his scooter. What he needed now was escape.

He ran a stop sign, then another, and the Hyundai did, too, but then both of them had to slow down because traffic picked up.

Pedestrian traffic, that is. Lots of it, and getting thicker all the time. Banners fluttered overhead and an unmistakable buzz filled the air. There was some kind of parade going on in town. Detour signs led to the right, and he was about to follow them when Mia tapped his shoulder.

"Dia di Rincon!"

"Dia di what?"

"There! That way!" She pointed into the mass of people.

Of course — they could lose themselves in the crowd. He slalomed around the barrier and glanced back to see the Hyundai squealing to a halt. Nearly did a fist pump, too, but it took all he had to keep the moped moving through the ever-growing crowd. Three meaty ladies in white-and-purple flounced skirts sashayed along in front of him. Men in Panama hats and striped shirts danced alongside bands and more ladies — many more ladies dressed very much like the Chiquita Banana girl without the bananas. With their colored ribbons, bouncing skirts, and towering hats, they looked like giant dancing fruit tarts topped with whipped cream.

"What is this?" he murmured, tiptoeing the bike around four women in dresses that reminded him of tropical birds.

"*Dia di Rincon!* The festival!"

It was a giant street party, a touch of Rio brought to one small town — or how he imagined Rio to be, at least. Spices wafted from sidewalk grills and filled his nostrils. Chatter, announcements, and the beat of drums thrummed in his ears. It was getting harder and harder to make any headway, so he turned down a side alley, then another, and another that widened and spit them out on a blissfully open road where he could hit the gas again. The wind whipped his hair as he counted the miles — er, kilometers.

"I think we lost them!" Mia cried.

He checked the side mirror, sure she'd just jinxed them, but no, the road was empty. Closed, by the look of it. Maybe they really were in the clear.

They zipped past a scrubby landscape that stretched mile after mile, and he counted every one. They'd hit a rise and catch a view of Kralendijk ahead, then bottom out in sandy valleys where tight rows of cacti created a living fence, hemming them in from both sides.

He pushed the engine as if the Hyundai were still hot on their heels, which it probably was, in a way. He figured the two men had taken a parallel road and were speeding along on a converging route. Somewhere ahead there'd be a juncture where they'd find the thugs lying in ambush if he didn't hurry along.

The moped's balance shifted slightly as Mia craned her head around. "Do you hear that?"

"What?"

He checked the mirror. Nothing.

"That."

He squinted at the long straightaway ahead. Nothing. Nothing in the mirror, either, but she was right. A distant buzz sounded from somewhere ahead.

"Too loud to be the car," he yelled over his shoulder. "And coming from the wrong direction."

"Maybe a truck?"

He was about to say *whatever*, because a truck heading out of town was the least of their problems, but as the moped sweated up a rise, a shadow fell over them. He looked up and saw a huge bird rising over the crest of the hill. It roared and dove right at them.

"Oh, shit!" Mia's arms tightened so quickly, he lost a breath.

Not a bird. A helicopter. Coming right at them.

He ducked and swerved just as it thundered over their heads, so close he felt his hair flatten from the wind or maybe even the skids.

"What the...?" he blurted, accelerating over the rise. The bad guys had reinforcements? "Where'd they get a helicopter?"

"One of the resorts?" Mia yelled into the wind. "Developers, remember?"

He glanced up and saw a pink flash. The helicopter had the same hibiscus logo painted on its side that the Hyundai had. Maybe Celeste's cousin the hairdresser was right. Maybe there really was a powerful developer behind the bombing of *Neptune's Revenge*.

The sleek, black chopper soared back into view and barreled straight at them, this time from behind. He swerved so hard the moped nearly spun out. The foot he stuck out to keep them upright skidded along the road fast enough to send heat searing through the sole. The backwash of the rotor plucked at his hair.

The helicopter raced ahead, rose in a wide, gravity-defying arc, and came back for another pass. Ryan started slaloming for lack of a better option with the fifty feet of maneuverable space defined by the twin walls of cacti on either side.

Mia screamed as the helicopter swept by in another pass, so close he could have grabbed a skid and swung up into the cockpit with one hand.

But he didn't want to get in that helicopter. He wanted to get himself and Mia as far away from it as possible, and now.

He stuck out a foot and somehow, somehow kept the moped from wiping out into cactus, then jerked the handlebars to get them back on course.

Mia stuck a hand over his shoulder. "There! Go!" she yelled.

As if he had some other choice.

Then he got it and accelerated toward the tree Mia was pointing at. Both of them leaned forward like they were on a galloping steed and not a purple scooter about to bust a hose. Behind him, the hum of the helicopter said it was banking into a turn, and the change in pitch of its rotor meant it was charging again.

"Come on, come on," he willed the scooter along.

He didn't have to look at the mirror to feel the helicopter bearing down on them, to sense the dragon's breath of its wash. His ears filled with the roar of it until he was sure that, this time, they were shit out of luck.

The roar became a screech as the helicopter peeled away. Miracle of miracles, they'd made it into the tiny shelter under those low-hanging branches where no helicopter would dare range. He put both feet down, coming to a standstill for the first time in what seemed like days.

"God, I could hug this tree," Mia murmured. She seemed to settle for tightening her grip around his waist, though, which suited him just fine.

The helicopter buzzed around the tree like a hornet, then hovered a short distance away.

"What now?" Mia croaked.

Were they calculating? Plotting? Loading rocket launchers?

The tree offered a measure of safety, but its branches were a cage. There was nowhere to go, nowhere to hide. And to make things worse, another engine sounded in the distance. Ryan jerked his head left to trace the noise.

This time it was a truck. He eyed it closely. Was it a big, lumbering truck innocently heading to town or a big, lumbering truck on a mission to flatten him and his mermaid? He revved the scooter engine, just in case.

The truck rolled past without the driver so much as batting an eye.

"Go!" Mia thumped him on the shoulder. "Follow it!"

God, she was smart. The helicopter wouldn't attack them in front of witnesses, or so he hoped. He twisted the throttle, darted after the truck, and steered the scooter in close — too close for comfort, really, but it beat getting beheaded by a helicopter — and hung in there, stealing glances in the mirror.

"What's the chopper doing?"

Mia twisted around. "The guy hanging out the side is talking into a radio."

A radio. Shit. They were probably calling out backup, like maybe a tank.

The truck slowed and joined a larger road with him and Mia in tow.

"Oh, great," Mia muttered.

"What?"

"The good news or the bad news?"

He shook his head. Why couldn't there just be good news? "Bad first."

"The Hyundai's back there again."

He glanced in the mirror and caught a glimpse of the pink and white Hyundai hurtling around a curve in the coastal road behind them. It disappeared behind a bend, but only momentarily.

"And the good news?"

"The helicopter is peeling away."

He glanced up, spotted a blur. "Why do I have the feeling these guys are tag teaming us?"

"Because they are? Because someone ambitious enough to bomb an internationally recognized ship has the resources to come up with a chopper and a car?"

Yeah, he guessed so.

"More good news." She tapped his shoulder as the truck ahead of them turned down a side road. "Look!"

They were approaching Kralendijk fast, and man, he'd never been so glad to arrive in a one-horse town in his life.

Then Mia muttered. "Oh, Jesus."

Now what?

"Cruise ship day." Her hand snaked over his shoulder, pointing out two huge ships moored just off the town. Ships that must have come in overnight.

"Good? Bad?"

"Crowds," Mia said. "Big crowds. Kralendijk gets to be a madhouse."

He tightened his grip on the handlebars. A madhouse. How fitting.

He didn't have much time to come to any conclusion, because they were within town limits now, and the Hyundai was gaining, and it was getting tight. Very tight.

They zoomed into the old town, with its white-trimmed colonial buildings painted in sunny yellows, bright blues, and rich oranges, all upbeat and cheery. He might have felt that way, too, if it weren't for the clueless tourists wandering the roads — the *roads*, damn it, not just the sidewalks — and the sedan looking to kill him very, very soon.

On the bright side — and Ryan was trying hard to find a bright side — he knew exactly where the police station was. Knew it all too well, unfortunately. He hammered down the main road as fast as he dared, cut a sharp left, then a right, slowed to a near crawl for an elderly couple taking pictures — pictures! — in the middle of the street, and finally sped up again. Up ahead stood the blue and white building that was police headquarters. They were nearly there. Surely the two men in the Hyundai wouldn't follow them that far, right?

The crazy thing was, they did, apparently hell-bent on eradicating him and his sailor chick from the face of the planet at any cost. On the other hand, their pursuers had problems of their own, now that a police car with flashing lights had pulled in behind them, making this a three horse race. Or rather, a two-horse, one-pony race, because the scooter was starting to overheat.

"The police know we're the good guys, right?" Mia muttered.

He kept his mouth shut.

They were so close to police headquarters, he could see the insignia on the flags fluttering ahead. Just as they got close, though, came a detour sign, and he skidded to a halt.

"Detour?" Mia yelped.

"Run for it!"

They jumped off the scooter and did just that, because the inside of the police station seemed like a much better place to do all the explaining they had to do than out here in shooting range. Yes, shooting range, because he caught a glimpse of one man leaning out of the Hyundai's window, pointing a gun.

Shit. A gun?

He turned in midstep to look back, and yes, there was the guy, swinging the barrel in his direction and taking aim.

"Hey! Stop!"

His head whipped around to where four people had run out of police headquarters to join the two officers stationed outside, all of them shouting and waving like mad.

He was running full tilt with Mia half a step ahead, but everything went into a slow-motion blur in his mind.

Cops ahead. No guns. And one of them, strangely, was a guy who looked a hell of a lot like Lucky.

Behind, two men with guns. Guns taking aim.

He glanced again. Shit — taking aim at Mia, not him.

Looked ahead. Too far to any kind of shelter.

He pictured the safety coming off the gun, a finger squeezing the trigger.

"Stop!" one of the policewomen yelled.

No time to stop. No time to think.

He launched himself at Mia and threw her to the ground a split second before the crack of a gunshot ripped through the air.

A burning sensation ripped through his arm.

He pushed the sensation aside and concentrated on rolling. Bumping. Keeping his body between Mia and the gunman even as the burning sensation turned to a dull ache that spread through his chest. They lurched to a stop and he hauled Mia up, shoving her behind the shelter of a parked car and diving in after her as more shots rang out. Shots from both directions, because it seemed the cops were armed, after all.

Mia swore. The cops yelled. Bullets pinged, but all of it seemed strangely muted.

"Ryan?" he heard her cry. Why did she sound so far away?

"Ryan!" she screamed.

Everything dimmed until all he could see was a splotch of an oil stain on the road, right in front of his nose. He blinked at it once. Twice. Then everything faded to black.

Chapter Twenty-Three

Three days later...

"Oh, Stanley, not another video!"

Mia wasn't the only one protesting. It was Thursday night in the bar, and Bruno, Marc, Dirk, and Anna were all waving Stanley away from the widescreen TV. Even Lucky and Hans groaned and turned away.

Everyone protested, except one man.

"This one's a special request," Ryan said from beside her, loud enough for everyone to quiet down.

Mia turned, sucking in a deep breath. It had been three days since the scariest moment of her life, and she still lost her breath looking at Ryan. Thinking of the near miss, the flood of relief that he was all right. The bullet had passed through the muscle of his arm but not ligament or bone, and not his heart, thank God. He was okay.

He'd waved away her tears in the hospital. *Nowhere near my heart,* he insisted even though his face was pale, his lips pinched. *Those guys had lousy aim.*

Sure, lousy aim. That's why Ryan had to rescue her for about the twentieth time in two days.

She reminded herself to breathe. Steady in, steady out. Ryan was okay, she was okay, everything was okay. The bandage on his right arm was proof of that, right?

She cupped his cheek in one hand, scraped a rough kiss over his mouth, then pulled back and squeezed his hand.

"Come on, Ryan. Let's call it a night."

It had been a long couple of days. One bad guy was dead, another behind bars, and an investigation was underway. According to Lucky, a special investigative team was tightening the noose around the group of investors who'd orchestrated the whole thing.

Lucky winked at her from across the table.

"I still can't believe you lied to me," Hans said to him.

"I didn't lie." Lucky shook his head. "I just left some things off my resume."

"Like being an undercover agent for the KLPD?"

KLPD. The Dutch secret service. One of the many things Mia had learned over the last few days.

Lucky shrugged like it was nothing. Like he hadn't been the one to save their lives by being quick on the draw that day in front of police headquarters.

"We had an anonymous tip about a threat to *Neptune's Revenge*, but we couldn't be sure what."

Mia snuggled closer to Ryan's side and ran a hand over his ribs. All okay. They were all okay.

"Come on, Ryan. Enough videos," she whispered. Home — *Serendipity* — had never looked so good, bobbing a short distance away on a nearby mooring. She and Meredith had sailed the boat back to town when the questioning was over. Ryan had been in the hospital, and she couldn't get her hands to stop shaking, but Meredith had been right. Sailing *Serendipity* did her good.

Meredith, her sister, the saint. She'd moved off the boat to house-sit for a friend of Celeste's, or so she claimed. Mia knew it was to give her and Ryan space. Time. Privacy. The chance to make up for lost time.

She hid a secret grin. Ryan had proven he was ready for that last night, and this morning too, and she couldn't wait for him to prove it all over again. Their own special kind of therapy for all they'd been through.

He'd kept his good arm slung over her shoulders all evening, and his fingers had strayed into adult-only territory more than once, so he seemed ready to call it a night, too. So why the sudden interest in yet another video? They'd seen hours of footage, helping the police hone in on the diver, his accomplice, and the launch caught in Stanley's video. Enough evidence to get the investigation headed on the right path, and more than enough to last her a lifetime. At least it had proven one thing: video did have its uses, after all.

Still, they'd all seen more than enough of Stanley's footage lately. She slid a hand over Ryan's thigh. Why was he so reluctant to get going?

He shot her a smile that looked a little forced. "This one is important. A special request. Ready, Stanley?"

"Just a sec," Stanley said, fussing with the TV.

"Good night, everybody," Marc waved, getting up with Bruno. "We're going to go."

"No," Ryan said, so forcefully half the room stared.

Mia, too. What had gotten into him?

"I need an audience," Ryan said softly. Soft and...sad, almost.

Before she could say anything, he pulled her to her feet, dragged a chair out in front of the TV, and pointed to it. "That's for you." Then he pulled out a second chair, turned it backward, and sat straddling it, facing the screen. His arms looped over the backrest and his head dipped a little bit. She'd never seen him look so tired or serious. What was so important about this video?

"A movie about police work in New York?" Hans asked, chuckling at his own joke.

"Sort of," Ryan murmured.

Stanley backed up, drawing everyone's focus to the black screen. It flickered with static then opened with an image of a plain white indoor wall. The drab image was the antithesis of everything Mia had been living in Bonaire: the vibrant reefs, the colorful houses, the tropical sky.

New York, she thought, placing the scene. That white wall was in a room in New York.

Something moved at the edge of the video, and first there was just a voice. Ryan's voice.

"Come on already, Murphy."

She glanced at Ryan, leaning forward over his chair with sad eyes glued to the screen.

A man stepped into the frame.

"Sit," Ryan's offscreen voice ordered.

The man sat awkwardly on a metal folding chair, looking everywhere but at the camera. He seemed familiar, but she couldn't quite place his face.

"Just start." That was Ryan again, sounding awfully military.

"Um... well..." Murphy squirmed like a little kid who'd been caught with the shattered remains of Grandma's vase.

"Say it already," Ryan's voice barked.

"So..." Murphy looked at a point to the right of the camera, where Ryan must have been standing while filming. "Her name's Mia, right?"

Her heart started thumping, low and foreboding. Everyone in the bar hushed and stared at her.

Ryan must have nodded to the man in the video, because he went on. "Right. Mia, I'm really sorry about that day..."

All the blood drained out of her face as she placed the face in the video. It was one of the policemen on the dive course that day in New York.

Murphy cleared his throat and started again. "I want to apologize for being such a jerk. I didn't mean... well... I didn't want..."

"Say it," Ryan barked from off-screen.

Murphy dragged his eyes to the camera, and it really felt like he was looking at her. Begging, almost. "I'm sorry for being such a dick. I'm sorry about what I said. I didn't mean to be disrespectful, but I was, and I'm sorry. Really sorry, and I hope... Well, I hope you don't hold it against Hayes, because he didn't say anything about anything that day."

That day. That hellish day at the dive course when Ryan's colleagues had made crude comments. The day she'd decided she never wanted to see him again.

Mia stared at him. Real Ryan, a yard away from her in a bamboo chair, his hands clutched tight. His face was grim and fixed steadfastly on the screen.

What was it he'd said to her way back when on Hans' dive launch?

I came to Bonaire to apologize. She blinked at the video.

Holy shit. He hadn't been kidding.

"Ken, you're next." The words pulled her attention back to the video, where poor Murphy — and she really did feel sorry for him now — filed off screen and a different man filed on. The one with the huge smile and cackling laugh, except he wasn't smiling or laughing now. He looked serious, dead serious.

"Mia," the man — Ken — started, and it was like he was right there in the hushed bar. "I said some pretty inexcusable things that day." His Adam's apple bobbed as he groped for words. "I wish I hadn't, but I can't take them back now. We didn't think it was..." He glanced around. "We didn't know it was you, and we didn't mean it the way it sounded. It was just...just messing around, and it was dumb. I'm sorry."

"Say it like you mean it," Ryan snapped from off-camera, and Ken shrank a little.

"I do mean it! I'm sorry!" Somehow, the thick Long Island accent made him sound doubly sincere. "It's just... I get it, Mia. Well, I think I do. I get that it hurt. But believe me, I won't ever do it again. Not to you or anyone else, in front of them or behind their backs."

It went on like that, one big tough guy after another looking small and almost pitiful in his regret. Then the last guy finished, and Ryan came on the screen.

Mia gulped.

Ryan took a deep breath and opened his mouth. Closed it again. Cleared his throat. Unlike the others, though, he didn't squirm, hem, or haw. He looked right into the camera. Right at her.

She wanted to reach out and touch him, to tell him he didn't need to do it, but it was too late. He'd already gone and done it — humbled himself in front of the men who respected him most.

For her. He was doing it for her. And he'd done it long before she bawled him out about not knowing what it felt like to be humiliated in public or to bare his soul.

And there he was, in the flesh and on screen, about to do just that in front of two audiences: his police squad in New York and the dive group huddled in Rick's bar, hushed and solemn as guests at a funeral.

"Mia," he said into the camera, clasping and unclasping his hands just as he did in the chair next to her in real time.

Everyone's eyes burned into her. She could feel it even as she stayed glued to the screen.

"We did a shitty thing." He shook his head and started again. "I did a shitty thing, and I can't take it back or make it go away." One cheek twitched, but his eyes were hard, like he was looking into a mirror and not a camera. "I wish I could, believe me, but I know I can't. I can't change what happened to you back then..." He waved, and she knew he meant before they met, when she was in college. "...and I can't change this, no matter how much I want to. I can only say I'm sorry and I mean it and it will never happen again. Even if you never let me see you again, I swear I'll remember how shitty it feels to make someone else feel like that."

Lots of words, she knew, from a man who preferred few. A good man who was trying very, very hard to set the record straight.

Ryan, she nearly whispered, *I get it*. She looked at him. *Enough*.

He stared at the camera long and hard, his soul shining in his eyes, begging for forgiveness.

Somewhere off by her left elbow, Hans cleared his throat. Gerta, his wife, sighed.

"I did a lot of things wrong," Video Ryan continued. "I'll probably mess up a lot more. But I want you to know that I won't mess up the same way. Not twice." He looked straight at the camera. "I swear."

His cheeks ballooned a tiny bit as he let out a puff of air, and the camera panned to show five bashful men, looking chagrined and penitent and sincere. Then the camera clicked off, and the screen went black.

Rick's Bar was quiet as the dead of night, like the times she woke up and came on *Serendipity's* deck to look at the stars and wonder.

Ryan sat there on his backward-facing chair, saying nothing, doing nothing. He rubbed a hand against his cheek and stared at the blank screen.

And Mia, she couldn't quite move or think.

It was Hans who broke the silence. He stepped to the bar and came back with two drinks. One, he put on an empty chair by Ryan's knee, and the other he raised in a silent toast. Ryan looked up and managed a pencil-thin imitation of a smile, and gradually, the bar patrons started whispering again. It was over, Mia realized. Except for one thing.

She stood up on shaky sea legs, wobbled over to his chair, and took his hand. It was slow motion at first, because she wasn't sure what to say or do, but then she got a little momentum going. Enough to pull him out of that chair and over by the water, away from the others. She sat him down and pulled out a second chair to face him, then thought better of that and sat in his lap, because she needed that proximity.

She looped an arm over his shoulders and leaned in until they were nose-to-nose like a couple of dogs or dolphins or whatever kind of animal that knew how to communicate without words. She rubbed her nose slowly up and down the length of his. Once, twice, then over his left cheek. She followed the line of his jaw right around to the other cheek. When she continued on that side, he nuzzled back and tightened his arms around her waist.

He opened his mouth, but she raised her fingers and beat him to it. "I think you've made it up to me, Ryan."

He shook his head. "I can never make it up. Not the way I want to."

She shook her head right back. "There are lots of things I would do differently if I could go back in time." She ran one finger down his cheek, bringing his mouth up for a kiss. "But some things, I wouldn't change at all."

She kissed him, open and honest and as sure as she'd ever been of anything in her life. She kissed until his mouth was moving, too, and everything was all right again.

"So now that you're done apologizing," she murmured, once they'd come up for air. "You think you might find time for funner things?"

The corners of his mouth turned up two or three degrees. "Funner? Like what?"

"Like some more of this," she mumbled, catching his lips again. "And this," she said, running a hand down the flat planes of his chest, along the rocky terrain of his stomach, and then barely, just barely into the top edge of his shorts. They were in public, after all. But not for long, she hoped. God, did she hope.

His green eyes were filled with smiles and ideas and hopes, like so many mysterious packages wrapped under a tree.

"And this," he added, pulling her against him in a crushing hug. His nose ruffled her hair when he mumbled again. "Just this."

Epilogue

One week later...

"Coming?"

Ryan popped his head out of *Serendipity's* cabin, looking toward the stern where Mia stood dripping on the swim ladder, urging him along.

"Hurry up!"

Like he was going to hurry a morning like this, even though he'd had a whole week of them now. Mornings waking up to no alarm but the sun, with nothing to rush off to except for Mia. And she was always right there, where she'd fallen asleep the night before, waiting for him.

"Such a New Yorker. Always in a rush," he scolded, coming up on deck.

He had to squint, not just from the morning sun bouncing off the water but because she'd been skinny-dipping. Her skin was glistening and her hair too, and Christ, how was a guy supposed to get excited about snorkeling when he could just look at that? To look at that and know part of her glow was his doing, and that he could keep right on doing it, because they had trust and understanding and a lot of other words that hadn't been in his vocabulary before Mia came along.

"The fish are calling you," she giggled, motioning toward the water.

His dick was calling him, too, but it would have to wait just a tiny little bit.

157

Serendipity floated over water so clear it was like drifting in air, soft and dreamy and filled with a thousand dancing particles of light.

"Coming." He stripped off the shorts he'd put on so that at least breakfast was a halfway civilized thing. But there was no point swimming in them, because they'd only get wet, and there was nobody around. Not for miles, it seemed.

She pushed backward, splashed into the water, and came up in that head-tilted-back move he loved so much, sending a hundred salty rivers streaming down her face. "You think we can talk Hans into letting us use this mooring forever?"

He chuckled, because Mia had Hans wrapped around her pinky, and she didn't even know it. Hans had permits for a dozen moorings around Bonaire and wasn't planning on bringing a group out to this particular one any time soon.

"Maybe he'll let us use it for five more weeks." He grinned, because five weeks off work felt like a cardinal sin. But getting shot, even thousands of miles away from New York, had to get you something. Between medical leave and the two weeks of unpaid personal leave he'd been granted, he and Mia had plenty of time to sort things out.

He jumped into the cool water feet first because he couldn't get his arm all the way over his head yet, even if the wound had closed up enough to let him swim. No scuba diving, but neither of them was in any rush for that.

Mia paddled in a circle when he came up, looking up at the boat. "I wish my granddad could see this," she sighed.

He chuckled and gave her a little pat on the rear. "Maybe not all of this."

She splashed him. "Okay, maybe not skinny-dipping with Officer Love, but the rest."

"Officer who?"

She doggie-paddled closer and gave him a sloppy kiss. "Officer you."

Their legs intertwined, and for a minute, he contemplated throwing her over his shoulder and dragging her back to his lair.

"You mean I have to suffer through five more weeks of this?"

She shook her head. "No, you only have to suffer through three more weeks of this. For two weeks after that you get to help Meredith and me sail *Serendipity* to Grenada. If you're still game."

"Wouldn't miss it for my life, lady."

Grenada. A month ago, he couldn't have aimed a dart at a map. Now, you could blindfold him and he'd be able to point the way because, yes, he and Mia had managed something other than long coffee breaks between marathon sex sessions these last couple of days. They'd studied the map and weather charts like they were the Bible, which to sailors, they were. So he knew exactly where Grenada was and what lay in the four hundred miles in between. A week, give or take, of sailing into the wind on a thirty-two-foot boat with Mia and her sister.

Yes, her sister. Which was okay, because it still beat what he'd put up with in the Navy by a fair bit. And anyway, by then he and Mia would have burned off some of the primitive energy force that had them shagging like bunnies day and night, right?

She brushed up against him and he caught a breath. Maybe. Maybe not. But they'd at least have burned off *enough* of it to last to landfall. And anyway, Meredith was a true champ, letting him and Mia play house on *Serendipity* for a while.

"Seriously, I'm happy house-sitting for a little longer," Meredith had said, and it even sounded true. "It lets me really experience Bonaire. You know, get to know the island a little better."

"Seriously?" Mia had asked.

"Sure." Meredith assured them again and again. So often, he wasn't all that sure any more. But then she'd perked up and whispered to Mia, "Celeste set me up on a date with her cousin. You think I should go?"

Mia had squeaked and given her two enthusiastic thumbs up. "I think you definitely should go."

So Meredith had set off on her own little adventure. A tamer adventure, Ryan hoped, than the one he and Mia had just survived.

"God, I hope she does okay this time," Mia had sighed, watching Meredith go.

"This time?"

Mia just shook her head. "It's a long story. A sad one." Her eyes followed her sister. "I hope she finally...well..."

He let her leave it at that. Meredith was allowed to keep her secrets, even if he and Mia had sworn off their own.

"Five weeks with you, wherever they are, are good with me," he murmured, pulling Mia into another slippery hug. "As long as I get lots of weeks after that, too."

"Weeks?" she protested.

"Months. Years." He kissed her between every word. "Decades."

"Sounds good," she whispered into the little space between their faces.

Yeah. Decades, at least.

He went to kiss her again but she was talking again.

"I hope the guy at City Divers wasn't kidding when he said they'd have an opening."

"Mia, the owner is pregnant. She can't dive, and they have a load of summer courses lined up. So yeah, I'm pretty sure they'll have an opening. They know you're great, and you're getting a great recommendation from Hans."

She laughed. "Getting a recommendation from Hans is like getting a recommendation from my dad. It hardly counts."

"It counts. Believe me, it counts. And it sounded like City Divers wants to run more trips to Bonaire if they could staff them."

Her eyes shone. "Yeah, that would be cool. A trip down here from time to time. You think you could swing it?"

He tucked his face alongside hers. "From time to time."

She hugged him tighter. "I could do that for a while. City Divers. Regular trips to great locations. A decent enough salary...for now."

"For now?" He cocked an eyebrow at her.

"Until you're ready to leave New York and try out that job in Florida." She knew about Plan B because he'd told her, because he'd made damn sure not to keep minor details from her any more.

He squeezed her hands. "Two more years, baby. Two more years." Two more years ought to be enough to truly deserve being called New York's Finest and gracefully bow out. Two more years of both of them saving, and they ought to have just enough to buy in to his buddy's salvage operation. He and Mia both.

But they'd cross that bridge when they came to it. This was perfect for now. More than perfect, in fact.

When she breathed in, her whole body rose, and when she exhaled, it was in another happy sigh that ended with her slipping backward just a little bit. She held up the masks and snorkels dangling in one hand as she treaded water beside him. "Maybe we ought to get snorkeling."

He pulled her back into a kiss. A full-body kiss that ran from his lips to his toes, because really, what was the rush?

"Eventually," he breathed at some point into another marathon kiss.

Her lips curled under his as she mumbled semicoherently. "Eventually."

Yes, *eventually* was the kind of clock he'd be happy to work by for the next month or so.

"No rush," he managed.

"No rush," she sighed and wound a leg around his, squeezing her hips to his.

"You kill me, Mia."

"In the best possible, way, right?"

He wanted to laugh, but his chest was all tight. It seemed like one of those times he ought to tell her just how good life was, but he struggled — as usual — to find the words.

Mia, though, seemed to read his mind again, because she smiled into his lips. "I get it, Ryan," she mumbled. "I get it."

A note from the author

I hope you've enjoyed your adventure on Bonaire! In case you're tempted to pull out a map, let me fess up to the facts. While some places in this story are described just the way you'll find them on your next trip to the Caribbean, others stem entirely from my imagination. So you can send me a postcard from Kralendijk and enjoy the festivities at Rincon (every year on April 30th), but don't spend too long searching for Wilhelm's Baai or the wreck of the *Henry Aalders*, except in the pages of this book. Otherwise, *bon voyage* — on your trip to the Caribbean, or on your next armchair adventure romance!

Sneak Peek: Adrift

Just another crazy day in paradise... Meredith Whitman isn't in the sunny Caribbean looking for trouble, especially not in the form of the Russian Mafia. All she wants is to contemplate enough tropical sunsets to forget the tragedies of her past. Still, trouble is what she gets – along with a second chance at true love.

Toussaint "Tuss" Anderson is a man on a mission that doesn't involve rescuing damsels in distress. But when bullets start to fly, he finds himself face to face with the one woman he can't get out of his mind. Now he's in the line of fire, too, and pitted against a ruthless foe. Can he help Meredith outfox a deadly criminal? And can he do it without sacrificing his life – or his love-struck heart?

Books by Anna Lowe

Serendipity Adventure Romance

Off the Charts

Uncharted

Entangled

Windswept

Adrift

Travel Romance

Veiled Fantasies

Island Fantasies

Spellbound in Sedona

Wind Whisperer (Book 1)

Fire Dancer (Book 2)

Dream Weaver (Book 3)

Sherwood Forest Shifters

Tempting the Sheriff (Book 1)

Tempting the Outlaw (Book 2)

Tempting the Maiden (Book 3)

Aloha Shifters - Jewels of the Heart

Lure of the Dragon (Book 1)

Lure of the Wolf (Book 2)

Lure of the Bear (Book 3)

Lure of the Tiger (Book 4)

Love of the Dragon (Book 5)

Lure of the Fox (Book 6)

Aloha Shifters - Pearls of Desire

Rebel Dragon (Book 1)

Rebel Bear (Book 2)

Rebel Lion (Book 3)

Rebel Wolf (Book 4)

Rebel Heart (A prequel to Book 5)

Rebel Alpha (Book 5)

Fire Maidens - Billionaires & Bodyguards

Fire Maidens: Paris (Book 1)

Fire Maidens: London (Book 2)

Fire Maidens: Rome (Book 3)

Fire Maidens: Portugal (Book 4)

Fire Maidens: Ireland (Book 5)

Fire Maidens: Scotland (Book 6)

Fire Maidens: Venice (Book 7)

Fire Maidens: Greece (Book 8)

Fire Maidens: Switzerland (Book 9)

The Wolves of Twin Moon Ranch

Desert Hunt (the Prequel)

Desert Moon (Book 1)

Desert Blood (Book 2)

Desert Fate (Book 3)

Desert Heart (Book 4)

Desert Rose (Book 5)

Desert Roots (Book 6)

Desert Destiny (Book 7)

Sasquatch Surprise (Book 8)

Desert Yule (a short story)

Desert Wolf: Complete Collection (Four short stories)

Blue Moon Saloon

Perfection (a short story prequel)

Damnation (Book 1)

Temptation (Book 2)

Redemption (Book 3)

Salvation (Book 4)

Deception (Book 5)

Celebration (a holiday treat)

Shifters in Vegas

Paranormal romance with a zany twist

Gambling on Trouble

Gambling on Her Dragon

Gambling on Her Bear

Gambling on Her Panther

www.annalowebooks.com

About the Author

USA Today and Amazon bestselling author Anna Lowe loves putting the "hero" back into heroine and letting location ignite a passionate romance. She likes a heroine who is independent, intelligent, and imperfect – a woman who is doing just fine on her own. But give the heroine a good man – not to mention a chance to overcome her own inhibitions – and she'll never turn down the chance for adventure, nor shy away from danger.

Anna loves dogs, sports, and travel – and letting those inspire her fiction. On any given weekend, you might find her hiking in the mountains or hunched over her laptop, working on her latest story. Either way, the day will end with a chunk of dark chocolate and a good read.

Visit AnnaLoweBooks.com